A Golden Christmas

A Collection of Holiday Themed Short Stories

By Jay Quin & Kay Andy

Christmas Be Good This Year

The hustle and bustle of the restaurant is a welcomed distraction for the woman as she carries a round tray filled with empty drinking glasses on the palm over her olive hand. Her mahogany hair swings in a short ponytail at the back of her oval-shaped head as she steps around the corner into the brightly lit commercial kitchen.

"Hey, how's the night going for you, Leah?" Another woman with caramel skin asks.

Leah shrugs her slim shoulders. "It's going as well as can be expected two days before Christmas."

The woman huffs out a breath and rolls her brown eyes. "Shouldn't these people be at home spending time with their family? Why are they fine dining tonight?"

"Kendall, if they weren't fine dining tonight, then we wouldn't be making any tips. I don't know about you, but I need all the money I can get."

Kendall grimaces, "My bad. I didn't think about that. I bet Brett and Kyle have a long Christmas list."

Brett and Kyle are Leah's twin ten-year-old sons. She's been raising them on her own since the day they were born. As a single mom, more often than not it's a challenge simply to make sure all the bills are paid on time. That is especially true when the holidays roll around. Leah hates disappointing her sons, but buying everything they want for Christmas and paying the bills cannot coexist. She regularly works two jobs, but still it isn't always enough.

This year she took on a third part-time job for the holiday season just so she can have a little extra for the two gifts Brett and Kyle agreed on - a television for their bedroom and a Nintendo Switch. Some people would say that those items aren't expensive. At least, that's what her arrogant brother said when he overheard her conversation with their mom. Of course, he's the kind of person that buys his bratty eight-year-old daughter what she screeches for. Life isn't fair that way. Brett and Kyle are great kids. Leah never has any trouble with them. They're obedient, neat, and they do well in school. Just once she wants to be able to give them what they asked for instead of what she can afford. She knows the material things don't matter, but her children's happiness does. They've never complained when they haven't gotten what they wanted, so in Leah's mind, that means they deserve to get what they're asking for even more.

"Their list isn't long at all," Leah responds to Kendall. The two are what some refer to as work best friends, but they don't usually socialize when they're not on the clock. Kendall is a college student who is working to afford her $50 monthly phone bill, gas for her car, and weekends at whatever bar she and her friends choose. She and Leah don't have much of anything in common when they aren't working together.

"I couldn't imagine being responsible for another human being, or two," Kendall murmurs.

"If you keep doing the things you're doing, you will be," Hannah, the shift manager, comments as she flicks her faded golden blonde hair off her shoulder. She's a middle-aged woman who's been working in the food service industry since before she graduated from high school. There's usually a scowl on her square wrinkled face.

Kendall shivers and pushes away from the chrome table she's leaning against. "Don't speak that negativity into my life. No offense to the two of you, but motherhood seems like a medieval concept that devours your will to live." It's not the first time she's said something along the line.

Leah lifts a serving tray that's loaded with the meals for one of her tables. "I love my sons. I wouldn't trade them for anything in the world." Carefully, she walks out of the kitchen into the dimly lit dining room.

The restaurant she's working at is one of those places that has three dollar signs beside its name on any search engine. It's rare that you'll see a customer wearing jeans when they dine here. The cheapest bottle of wine on the menu costs fifty dollars. With the low hourly wage and customer tips, the employees make barely enough to get by.

Leah delivers the food to her waiting customers. "Can I get you anything else?" she politely asks. The elderly couple shakes their heads silently dismissing her. She walks past her other two tables that have diners and covertly cheeks to see if they're in need. They appear to be happy eating their meals, so she walks to the host's desk.

"It's kind of slow tonight," the host, Melvin, comments as he rolls silverware into white cloth napkins.

Leah frowns as glances around the dining area. "Let Kendall tell it, it's too busy."

Melvin scoffs, "That girl is just trying to get out of here early."

The golden framed door opens and a tall man wearing a dark gray suit walks inside. He grins as he sees Leah standing by the host desk.

His diamond-shaped head tilts to the right. "How did you know I was coming?" The man is Garret Sheffield. He's one of the most successful attorneys in the state and he also happens to be a regular customer at the restaurant. He usually sits at one of Leah's tables.

"I didn't," Leah responds with a laugh. "You haven't been around in a while."

Garret shrugs his broad shoulders. "I've been busy with work." He looks at Melvin and nods his head in greeting. "How have you been? How's your wife doing?"

"I've been working a lot. My mother-in-law is in town," Melvin responds with a grimace.

Garret matches his facial expression. "Hopefully she'll leave soon."

"She's staying for my wife's birthday."

"When is that?"

"The eighth of January," Melvin answers in a deadpan voice.

"Oh man, I'll keep you in my thoughts," Garret chuckles.

Leah grabs a menu and silverware. "You can follow me to your table." They walk in comfortable silence to the small round table. Garret sits in one of the scroll-backed chairs. "Do you want your regular drink?"

"Yeah, that's fine. How have you been?"

"I've been as good as I can be," Leah huffs. "I'll go get your drink while you look over the menu."

When Leah walks into the kitchen, Kendall playfully nudges her. "Melvin said your boyfriend is here."

Leah rolls her eyes. "Garret is not my boyfriend."

Hannah frowns. "He didn't become a regular customer until you started working here, and he doesn't like it when anyone else serves him."

"That's not true," Leah denies as her cheeks redden. Garret is an attractive man with light golden skin, chocolate curly hair that he keeps cut short, and crater-like dimples in his cheeks. His voice is rich with vibrato.

"Yes, it is," Kendall sings. "He hasn't been around lately. Did the two of you have an argument or something?"

"I don't argue with customers. He said he's been busy with work." Leah walks out of the kitchen to the bar to order Garret's usual drink - whiskey and coke over ice.

Kendall follows her. "Have the two of you exchanged numbers yet?"

"No, that would be inappropriate."

The young waitress smacks her lips together and rolls her eyes. "No, what's inappropriate is that way he watches you walk away."

"Kendall," Leah gasps. "You need to lower your voice. You can't say things like that. You may get me fired."

"Hannah doesn't care. You're the only one being uptight about it."

"There's nothing to be uptight about. Garret is just a nice customer who happens to come here often. That's it."

Kendall folds her arms across her expansive chest. "Are you sure about that?"

"I am. He's a successful attorney from a family of successful attorneys, he would never be interested in someone like me. I barely graduated high school and I've never stepped foot on a college campus."

"I can't tell if you're blind or willfully ignorant. Either way, you're wrong. Garret likes you. Maybe he'll make his move soon."

Leah accepts the drink from the bartender. "I think you're the one who's wrong." She stops to check on her other customers before delivering Garret's drink. "Here you go. Are you ready to order your food?"

"I don't know. I've been looking at the holiday specials. Is the cranberry glazed turkey any good?"

Leah shrugs her shoulders. "I've never tried it, but some of my other customers ordered it tonight and they seem to like it. It looks good."

"Have you had your break yet?"

"Not yet."

"Have it now with me, and I'll order the turkey dinner for both of us." It's not the first time he's made this suggestion.

Leah puffs her cheeks as she glances around. "I'll have to get my other tables checked out and get permission from my manager."

"That's fine. We need time for the food to cook."

"You drive a hard bargain mister. I'll be back to check on you soon."

"Take your time. I'm going to make a call for work."

It's hard not to hurry as Leah politely asks her other customers if they would like to order dessert. When they decline and ask for their checks, she smiles and nearly bounces away from them. After the checks are paid and she's collected the tip from the tables, Leah enters the kitchen.

"Hannah, do you mind if I take my break now?"

Hannah's eyes narrow. "Do you have any seated tables?"

"Only Garret," she answers.

"In other words, he wants you to eat with him," Hannah correctly assumes. Leah silently nods her head in response. "Alright, take your break, but you'll probably be done for the night. We close in an hour and I don't think a lot of customers will come in before then."

"In that case, I'll go clean my section." Leah grabs the short broom and standing dustpan and walks to her section of tables. It takes a little over twenty minutes to wipe each of the tabletops, sweep, and refill the salt and pepper shakers.

Unbeknownst to her, Garret covertly watches as she works. He doesn't know what it is about the kind waitress that keeps him coming back to the overpriced restaurant. In the past nine months, he's come to the restaurant no less than twice a week. Even his mom has gotten suspicious as to why he's been eating here so often. He hasn't figured out a way to explain it to her. Truthfully, he doesn't know how to explain it to herself. The two weeks that he didn't come to the restaurant felt unnatural. He tried his hardest to get here sooner, but the jury trial he recently completed kept him busy well into the night. He barely made time to eat let alone to sit down in any restaurant.

A grin covers his face as Leah approaches the table carrying two dinner plates. Carefully she sits them on the table before smiling widely and dramatically motioning to the plates.

"Dinner is served," she mockingly announces.

Garret chuckles, "Thank you." He motions to the chair across from him. "I believe that seat belongs to you." He notices she's already taken off the black apron that all of the servers wear.

She holds up her hands with the palms facing him. "Before I get comfortable, do you need anything? Maybe another drink."

Garret hesitates, "Just one more."

She nods, "I'll be right back."

He watches her walk away with narrowed eyes and upturned lips. She leans against the bar and waves the bartender over. Seeing her smile as she speaks with the man makes Garret uncomfortable. He wonders if she's flirting with the man. Perhaps she likes him. Maybe they're involved. Leah is an attractive woman. He's certain that he's not the only one who has noticed that. Surely someone has expressed an interest in being romantically involved with her. Meanwhile, he's done nothing but monopolize her time while she's working.

Leah returns before he can spiral too far into his thoughts. She places the drink in front of him and takes her seat. He waits until she's had her first bite before he speaks.

"What's the verdict?"

"It's good," she speaks with her hand covering her mouth. "This was a good suggestion."

Garret lifts his fork and knife. "I'm glad you think so. One thing I do know is good food."

She giggles, "Is that so?"

"Is it. There's a little hole in the wall not far from here that has the best chicken wings in the country."

"Whoa, you know chicken wings are my territory," she interjects. He's teased her many times before about her choice of favorite food.

Garret playfully rolls his eyes. "Even you would enjoy this place. I'll take you there sometime. Your birthday is coming up." Her lips press together at his words. "Is there a problem?"

"Did you hear what you said?"

He shrugs his shoulders. "We're friends, right?"

Her mouth opens, closes, and opens again. "Yeah, we are."

"Friends help each other celebrate their birthdays. Are you opposed to seeing me outside of these four walls?"

She nibbles on her bottom lip before responding to him. "No, I'm not opposed to that."

"Good. Brett and Kyle can come along as well. How are they?"

"They're good," Leah answers with a frown.

"If that's the case then why are you frowning?"

It's her turn to shrug her shoulders. "It's nothing."

Garret shakes his head and points his fork at her. "You know nonchalance will not work with me. What's wrong?"

"For the first time that I can remember, Brett and Kyle have agreed on a Christmas gift."

"Is it a bebe gun?" Garret asks, referencing the boys' previous obsession with the item. They even went so far as asking their granddad for one. Leah made sure to tell her dad that under no circumstances was he allowed to buy her young sons something so dangerous.

She chuckles and shakes her head. "No, they let go of that when I stop my dad from getting them one for their ninth birthday."

"Well, that's good. What is it that they want this year?"

"A television for their bedroom and a Nintendo switch. I've been working more than usual which means that my car has decided that now is the time for the check engine light to come one. I'm going to have to use some of the extra money to take care of that. I was able to buy the game console, but I won't be able to get the television."

Garret looks at her with a soft look on his handsome face. "I'm sure they'll understand."

"They will, but I hate disappointing them. I feel like a bad mom."

"You are not a bad mom. You work hard and make sure your sons have everything they need."

"Obviously I don't work hard enough because they don't have everything they want."

His hand twitches with the urge to reach over for hers, but he refrains. "Not being able to give your kids everything they want does not mean you're a bad mom. They have a home, clothes, food, and they're happy. You're doing everything you're supposed to do."

Leah continues frowning as she wipes a stray tear away. "Thanks for saying that. It was nice."

"It was the truth," Garret insists.

They continue eating and talking about anything and everything. Garret is good at getting Leah to laugh. It's while she's holding her midsection from a funny story he told that Kendall comes to inform her that she's cut for the night. Leah hurries to finish eating so she can give Garret his check. As per usual, she doesn't charge him for her meal. Of course, he refuses not to pay.

"Keep the change," he instructs while handing her two hundred dollar bills.

She shakes her head at him. "I will not," she refuses.

"I'll leave before you can give it to me," he says while standing. "Thanks for the exceptional service."

"Garret, don't you dare leave," Leah calls after him as he walks away. He stops long enough to wave at her. Shaking her head, she walks away.

"Did he over tip again?" Kendall asks with a knowing smile.

"He does it every time," Leah grumbles.

"That's because he *loves* you." Kendall teases, waggling her eyebrows.

"Don't be ridiculous." Leah finishes her side work before clocking out and walking into the dark parking lot. She made sure to park close to the building because she knew she would be done with work close to the restaurant's nine o'clock closing hour. Hurriedly she unlocks her door and sits in the driver's seat. She sticks the key in the ignition and turns. Nothing happens. She tries again but the result is the same. "Are you kidding me?" Her voice nearly breaks as her hand slaps the steering wheel with frustration.

A knock on her window causes her to jump. Tightly gripping her taser, she turns only to see Garret standing expectantly beside her car. Cautiously, she opens the door.

"Having car trouble?" he asks.

Her bottom lip pokes out. "The light just came on today. I thought I had some time before it would need to be repaired."

"Well, it's cold and dark. You won't figure out what's wrong with it tonight. Let me drive you home."

"You don't have to do that."

"I know. I want to." He steps back and motions for her to follow him. Reluctantly, Leah locks her car. Garret's black Mercedes sedan is parked a few parking spots away. He holds open the passenger door for her and closes it before he walks around the car and gets in. "What's your address?"

"1021 Lee Parkway," she responds while pulling her cell phone out of her back pocket. She messages her babysitter, her sister, and lets her know that she's getting a ride home from Garret.

Carly: *What happened to your car?*

Leah: *The check engine light came on earlier and now it won't start.*

The drive to the three-bedroom house that Leah and her sister are renting doesn't take more than fifteen minutes. Garret parks in the cracked driveway while observing the faded yellow siding of the exterior. Yellow light glows in the windows.

"The boys must still be awake," Leah comments. Her younger sister isn't much of a disciplinarian.

"Can I meet them?" Garret surprisingly requests.

"Oh, um," Leah quickly tries to remember if her home is clean. "Yeah, I guess that'll be okay."

"If you're uncomfortable, I can wait."

"No, I'm fine. Let's go." She gets out of the car before she loses her nerve and changes her mind. The walk to the front door seemed like the longest of her life. A part of her wants to say never mind and tell Garret that he should leave. The other part of her feels like this has been coming for a long time. He's her friend. All of her other friends have met her sons. Surely it's time for him to meet them as well.

As soon as she opens the doors, her boys happily rush to her and nearly tackle her to the floor with a hug.

"Mommy! Mommy! We made you dinner," they exclaim.

Leah gasps, "You did?"

Simultaneously they nod their heads, but it's the one with bright yellow hair hanging over his forehead that speaks. "Aunt Carly will claim she did all the work, but we did the hard part."

A slim woman with brunette hair gathered in a messy bun on the top of her oval head walks into the entryway. "Kyle, the 'hard part' was putting the pan in the oven."

Kyle rolls his dark eyes. "It was hard! I almost burned myself." Carly and Leah laugh at his outburst.

The other boy with hair the same color as his mother and pale blue eyes nods his head. "Yeah! I supervised! It looked like it almost hurt him real bad." He's always ready to defend his brother even if it's against his own family. "Aunt Carly stopped him before he could, but--"

"Brett! Don't tell her that!" His twin covers the boy's mouth to stop him from uncovering the truth. An argument ensues, but neither the mother nor the aunt is surprised.

With a goofy grin on her face, Leah looks at Garret and shrugs her shoulders. "Boys, meet my friend." That is enough to draw their attention.

"Um, who are you?" Kyle demands with his mouth turned up.

"My name is Garret," the man calmly answers.

Brett folds his arms across his chest and glares at the newcomer. "What are you doing with our mom, *Garret*?"

"I gave her a ride home."

"Why?" they ask in unison.

Leah holds up her hands. "Whoa. Chill with the interrogation." She looks at Garret with apologetic eyes. "I'm sorry. They don't usually greet people like that."

"I'm guessing you don't usually bring men around them," Garret responds.

"Not since their dad," Leah admits sheepishly. "Most of my friends are women, so we don't usually have moments like this." As she speaks, the boys rush to the right where a small living room is situated.

"Come on, Mom, let's watch 'the Grinch'," Kyle calls out, patting the couch between him and Brett. "It's our *tradition*." He all but begs his mom.

"Oh, I don't know, boys. I'm really tired from work," Leah sighs and walks over to the couch, dramatically fainting on her twins.

"Ow! Get off!" They push at her but she doesn't move. A fond smile covers Garret's face as he watches.

"They're obnoxiously cute, right?" Carly asks, nudging him with her elbow. "They do this every night."

As Garret went to answer, a timer in the kitchen went off and the twins became even more determined to push their mom off.

"Dinner's ready! Mom, *move!*" Brett groans and breaks free, making a mad dash for the small kitchen.

"Let me get the pan out of the oven," Carly insists as she follows her nephew.

"No, I'm a man Aunt Carly. I've got this."

"Wow, he is something else," Garret laughs and goes to help Leah stand up off her second child.

"Thanks, strange man. She was crushing me," Kyle huffs.

"*Hey!*" Leah gasps in fake offense. "I'm not that heavy."

"That's what *you* think." Kyle runs off after his brother. "Hey, wait, let me help!"

"Both of you get out of the way so I can do it," Carly fusses.

Garret chuckles and shakes his head. "Is it like this every night for you?"

"Every. Night." Leah blows out a breath and looks around her living room. The boys' shoes are strewn around the space and the decorative pillows on the couch are in disarray. There's even a bowl of milk on the square faux wood coffee table. "I'm sorry this place is such a mess."

"If you think this is a mess, then you do not want to see my place," Garret jokes although there's a little seriousness to his voice. He's not the neatest man but his career has allowed him to afford to have a cleaner come into his home once a week to put it back in order. "I'm glad I got to meet Kyle and Brett. They're hilarious."

"They're resident comedians of Golden Shore, Virginia, but they keep me entertained." Before she can say anything else, the boys rush into the living room.

Kyle is holding the rectangular-shaped gold baking pan with oven mitts as Brett closely follows. "Look what we made." Inside the pan is a small whole hen that's been seasoned and baked to a warm golden brown color. "There's also brown gravy and mashed red potatoes like Great Nan used to make."

Leah's eyes fill with tears. "Oh, wow, thank you, boys." Her grandmother passed away at the beginning of the year and she's been less than enthusiastic about experiencing the first Christmas without the woman present. Leah's grandma was her biggest supporter. When Leah found out she was pregnant, her grandma was the first person she told. The older woman pulled her in a hug and made sure to tell Leah that she was still loved. Every year the night before Christmas Eve, Grandma would bake a hen and cook mashed red potatoes and invite her family over for dinner. When Leah got a job and started working, Grandma started hosting the dinner later at night so everyone could be together. It was a tradition that no one had the heart to continue when the woman passed away.

Carly tearily smiles at her sister. "They wanted to surprise you." She notices the confused look on Garret's face and explains the significance of the meal.

He clears his throat and carefully looks at the boys. "That was very sweet of you."

"Why don't the two of you go sit at the dining table with Aunt Carly and I'll join in a bit?" Leah suggests. Her voice is clogged with emotion. "Well, thank you for stopping by, but I'm sure you have other places to be." Leah clears her throat. "Thank you again, for the ride."

"The strange man can stay!" Brett calls from the kitchen. "We got him a plate and everything!" Garret chuckles and looks to Leah for confirmation.

"Well, the boys have spoken. Would you like to stay for dinner?" She asks, hoping he'd say yes.

"I'd love to. It smells delicious." It doesn't matter that they ate only a few hours before. He doesn't have the heart to turn down an invitation from Leah or her selfless sons.

Within seconds the dining room is filled with laughter and easy conversation between the five of them. It's mostly the boys asking the 'strange man' how he knows their mother. Carly's quick to join in the questioning and Leah can't hide her embarrassment. Eventually, she diverts their attention by discussing Christmas plans. Her parents are on a cruise, so this year it'll just be Leah, the boys, and Carly celebrating together. Soon, dinner ends, and the boys are fighting over who has to do the dishes.

"Thank you for staying." Leah walks Garret to the door, his coat hanging over her arm. "The boys loved you."

"Really? Do you think so? That's surprising. They kept calling me 'strange man'." He laughs and takes his coat from Leah.

"Hey, they kept talking to you. That's a win in my book." The pair linger by the door, not wanting to say goodbye just yet. "Well um," Leah finally breaks the silence. "I need to get the boys in bed. It's way past their bedtime and Carly is basically like a third child."

"Right, yeah of course." Garret clears his throat. "Thank you again for letting me stay for dinner." As he goes for a hug, Leah sticks her hand out to shake his. "Oh, sorry um... yeah." He smoothly takes her hand and gives her a firm shake. "Hey, if I don't see you beforehand, Merry Christmas."

"Merry Christmas." She smiles up at him and watches him walk out her front door.

He pauses and looks back at her. "I hope you don't mind me asking but what happened to their dad?"

Leah sadly smiles. "I don't mind you asking. He decided he would rather be a bigshot musician than be a father. It's for the best. From what the media shows, his life is a mess. I don't want Kyle and Brett involved in that."

Garret frowns, "You've never tried getting any financial support from him?"

"Nah, I don't need it. I can take care of my sons just fine."

"Yes, you can. It's his loss. He doesn't know what he's missing out on." Garret gives a half-hearted wave as he continues down the short staircase and to the driveway.

On the way to his car, he makes a decision. Leah and her family deserve everything they want and more. He can see how close they are and how much they love each other. They haven't had the easiest life. He wants to bring some happiness into their lives. He put the nearest department store into his GPS, hoping they'll still be open by the time he arrives.

~~*~~

Christmas morning is never peaceful for Leah. She always works late Christmas Eve and ends up scrambling to wrap last-minute presents and place them under the tree before the twins wake up and chaos ensues throughout the house. She finishes putting the stockings back up on the wall as she hears stirring coming from the twins' room.

"Brett! Come on, wake up!" She hears Kyle whisper harshly. "We gotta beat mom this year!"

"I don't wanna," Brett moans. "I want to keep sleeping."

Kyle loudly groans. "Come *on.*"

Leah laughs silently to herself as she lies back down on the couch, covering herself up to pretend to be asleep. The shuffling of feet sounds from the hallway and she closes her eyes. The twins are shushing each other as they walk up to the couch. They can't keep themselves from giggling as they count to three.

"Mommy!" They jump on top of Leah causing her to 'wake up' laughing as they crawl all over her to get her up off the couch.

"Okay, okay, I'm awake." She laughs and sits up, holding the boys in her arms as she does.

"Did you catch him this year?" Kyle excitedly asks.

Leah looks around the living room and pouts as she sees the evidence that Santa had been there the night before. "Darn, I didn't." She motions towards the empty plate and cup. "It's okay, I'll get him next year." She winks at her frowning twins.

"You say that *every* year." Kyle pouts and crawls off his mother's lap.

"And I mean it! I'm very serious about catching Santa Claus." She leans in close. "You know, I think he uses a special sleeping spell. That's why nobody's ever caught him." The boys' eyes widen and they turn to each other, already conspiring on how to catch him next year.

"What's for breakfast? I'm starving." Carly yawns as she makes her way down the hall from her room. "Merry Christmas, punks." She ruffles their hair as she passes them and makes her way to the kitchen.

"I haven't cooked yet," Leah informs her sister.

"Yeah, we just woke her up," Brett chimes in.

Carly gasps and spins around. "Did you catch Santa?"

"Not this year," Brett answers in a mumble. "But Mom is going to try again next year."

"I sure am," Leah agrees. Some people would say the twins are too old to believe in Santa Claus, but she likes that they still do. It gives them a little bit more innocence. "Okay, breakfast! I'll stick the cinnamon rolls in the oven and we'll get to opening presents."

Ten minutes later, Leah sits down on the floor with her boys and sister. "Alright, dinosaurs for Kyle, planets for Brett." Leah and Carly distribute the few gifts evenly between the twins and Leah brought out the big gift; the game station they had been asking for all year.

"No way!" Brett exclaims after they've ripped the wrapping paper off the box. "Mom, you're the best."

Carly laughs, "Buying your affection is so easy."

"Now, I couldn't get the TV just yet--"

"That's fine! We can connect it to the one in the living room!" Kyle smiles at his mom as Brett runs over to the family television to start setting it up. "Aunt Carly, turn on your hotspot. We need the internet."

"Demanding," Carly grumbles while doing as her nephew requested.

Brett quickly hugs Leah. "You deserve celebratory eggnog. I'll be right back." He rushes to the kitchen as there's a soft knock at the door causing the boy to divert his path. The sisters turn to look at each other.

"Now, who in the world is here at six in the morning? Are you expecting someone?" Carly raises an eyebrow.

"No, I thought maybe you were."

"Nah, all of my sneaky links know not to pop up at my crib. That's a one-way ticket to being cut off."

"Mom! The strange man is here!" Brett calls out from the front door and makes his way back to the kitchen.

"Strange man?" Leah stands up and grabs her robe off the end of the couch to inspect who this 'strange man' was.

"Yeah, the one from the other night."

She gasps, "Do you mean Garret?"

"Um, if that's the strange man's name, then yeah."

Her eyes widen. "Oh my God! He cannot see me like this." Leah frets as she rushes out of the living room in an attempt to get to her bedroom.

Carly stands as well. "I'll handle this." Happily, she makes her way to the door and pulls it open. "Merry Christmas Garret, come on in."

"You did not handle it!" Leah fusses, still trying to run away so she can hurriedly make herself presentable. Instead, she runs headfirst into Garret's wide back. "Oh, come on!"

He turns around to face her. "Um, good morning."

Leah shakes her head. "No, it is not a good morning. What are you doing here? You can't be here. You can't see me like this."

His eyebrows draw together in confusion. "What do you mean?"

"I look a mess. I haven't showered. My hair isn't combed. Oh my God, I need to stop talking. I haven't even brushed my teeth." She slaps a hand over her open mouth.

Kyle chuckles, "I haven't brushed my teeth since Tuesday."

Carly gags, "That is absolutely disgusting. What is wrong with you kid? Come on. I need to wash your mouth. Have you ever tasted bleach? It's a little sweet." She grabs his hand to try to pull him to the bathroom.

"I don't think bleach is necessary," Garret interjects.

"Oh, it's absolutely necessary. What do you know, *strange man*?" Carly rolls her eyes without letting go of her nephew.

Garret looks at Leah. "You leave *her* alone with your kids every day."

"Um, not every day," Leah mumbles. "Maybe I should start measuring the bleach." Leah snaps back to the conversation at hand. "What are you doing here? It's Christmas. You should be with your family."

"I'm on the way there now. But first I thought I'd drop off a few things." He grabs Leah's hand and leads her to her front door. "Ta-da!" His hands thrust outward, showcasing the large box sitting on the porch.

Leah gasps as she sees the brand new smart TV sitting on her porch. "Garret, you didn't."

"I did," he sings. He notices the glare she's directing at him. "I mean, *I* didn't. Santa did. He just somehow mixed up your address and mine."

"Then take it home."

"Absolutely not. It's heavy. My weak self could only carry it about as far as it is to your boys' room."

Leah crosses her arms over her chest and continues to glare up at the man. "How did you get it in your car? You told me you live in a high-rise apartment downtown."

"Actually, I live in my car."

"Then how do you have an address?" Carly asks just to add to the irrational conversation.

"Um," Garret stumbles with his response. "Leah, please. Your boys deserve this. *You* deserve to rest easy and not worry about what you couldn't get for them. I know you were stressed about this. Please. Let me help the boys set it up."

"At least let me pay you back for it."

"Absolutely not. Carly, help me carry this." Carly rushes to the front door and picks up one end of the box while Garret grabs the other.

"Do not help him," Leah orders.

"Sorry, my ears aren't working. So weird."

"Please tell me their room is close," Garret grunts as they hold the large box.

"Other end of the house, bud."

"Cool. Neat. Love that."

Leah narrows her eyes on her sister. "If your ears aren't working, then how did you answer him, Carly?"

"Huh? What'd you say?!" Carly leans forward and lowers her voice. "Let's move it, man. She terrifies me."

The two struggle to get the TV into the boys' room, but they somehow make it before the twins come out of the kitchen with the cinnamon rolls. "Done."

"What's done, strange man?" Kyle asks, his mouth full of the breakfast pastry.

"Oh, Santa came to me this morning with a gift for you two. I just set it up in your room. Want to see?" He motions down the hall and the twins start to run to their room.

"Careful! Not with your mouths full, you'll choke!" Leah calls after them.

"Oh, I can't go there but I want to so bad," Carly mutters as she walks to the living room. Leah glares at her. "What? If you don't, I will." Carly nods her head towards Garret.

"*Carly*!" Leah slaps her sister's arm. Garret walks up to the pair and hands them both a small box. "What's this?"

"What? You think I'd get your boys a gift and not the two of you?" Garret nudges Leah.

"You're determined to give me an ulcer," Leah heavily sighs.

Carly takes no time to open her gift. "Oh, my God. Thank you, Garret!" She hugs the tall man. Leah catches a glance at the golden hooped earrings with small diamonds on the outside of them. Leah's stress levels rose as she looked up at him.

"Okay, now you have to open your gift." Leah shakes her head and hands it back to him.

"It's too much."

"You don't even know what it is."

"I don't care. It's too much."

"Fine, then I'll open it for you." Garret insists and begins to tear back the wrapping paper on the gift.

"Garret--"

"Here," The man smiles and shows her the beautiful diamond necklace sitting in the Tiffany blue box. Leah's breath catches in her throat.

"No. No, no, no. I can't accept this. I told you it's too much--"

"No, it's not. Personally, I don't think it's enough." Garret shrugs and walks behind Leah to put the jewelry around her neck.

"Why did you buy this for me?" Her voice was thick with emotion.

Heavily he sighs but he doesn't respond. He waits until the necklace is clasped around her neck before he stands in front of her. Vulnerability fills his eyes. "My dad always says you should do everything you can to make the woman you love smile."

"You... I'm sorry, what?"

"Leah, I'm in love with you."

"Aww," Leah snaps her head around to see Carly casually leaning against the wall, hand over her chest.

"Oh, so you heard that all the way from the kitchen, but couldn't hear me tell you not to help him?"

"Huh? I can't hear a word you're saying but I think I can read your lips. I have selective hearing. I don't select what I hear. It's all up to my ears. I think there's something wrong. You know Dad dropped me a couple of times when I was a baby." Carly shrugs and pushes herself off the wall. "Don't leave the man waiting." She scoffs and makes her way back to her room.

"You don't have to say it back. I know it seems sudden, but--"

"I'm in love with you, too." Garret smiles and reaches for Leah's face, gently cradling it in his hand as he leans in for a kiss.

"*Ew!*" Leah pulls away from the almost-kiss to see her twins in the hallway making gagging faces. "Gross!"

"Are you about to kiss the strange man?" Brett asks with his mouth twisted and his eyes narrowed.

"His name is Garret," Leah reminds her son.

Brett's nostrils flare. "I don't care what his name is. I don't want to watch you two kiss."

"Then walk away," she suggests and turns back to Garret, pulling him in until their lips finally meet.

"That is so not okay," Kyle grumbles as he and his twin walk back to their bedroom.

Leah and Garret ignore the boy's commentary as they stand in the entryway allowing themselves to give in to their feelings for one another. For months they've flirted and admired each other from afar. Now the magic of the holiday has allowed them to set aside their worries and embrace their love. There's no doubt that they will always remember how good Christmas was this year.

All I Want for Christmas

"It has to be perfect," Lola insists, "it's our first Christmas as a married couple." She's looking over the gift options at the men's clothing store with dark scrutinizing eyes.

"Do you really think Josh will care that much about what kind of shirt you bought him, especially since you also bought him five other gifts?" Her brother, Tyler, asks as he walks beside her. Anyone who sees them together would probably think they were twins. They both have caramel skin, square faces, nearly jet black hair that hangs a couple of inches past their shoulders, and dark brown eyes with lids that sit low. In actuality, Tyler is three years younger.

Lola shrugs her round shoulders. "He might! Our first Christmas as Mr. and Mrs. Lopez will be remembered forever. Every gift that we give to each other must be meaningful."

"It's two days before Christmas. If you wanted a meaningful gift then you should have bought it sooner. You're acting like this is your first Christmas together *ever*. The two of you have been a couple for six years."

"Christmas as boyfriend and girlfriend, and Christmas as husband and wife are not the same."

"What about last year? You were engaged."

"Engaged isn't married," Lola huffs. "Why did you agree to help me if you're just going to complain the entire time?"

Tyler rolls his eyes at his dramatic sister. "I'm not complaining. I'm trying to talk some sense into you." Lola waves him off and goes back to her search in the shirts. "Does Josh know that you've spent nearly \$500 on gifts for him alone? I've got a feeling he won't be happy about that."

"Josh and I still have separate bank accounts until next month," Lola shrugs. "I've got my job and he has his. We've got plenty to cover our bills and groceries for the month. It's not a big deal."

"It's not a big deal?! You work at a daycare and he works in construction. The two of you aren't rich. Lola, please get your head on straight," Tyler groans and begins to massage his temples. "I won't let you stress me into an early grave."

"Calm down, Mr. Dramatic. I've got it covered." She scowls as she stops looking through the clothing racks. "Nothing here is catching my eye. Maybe we should go somewhere else."

"Or maybe you shouldn't buy anything else. He has other gifts from you already."

"Josh does so much for me... I just want to show him that I appreciate him, you know? I mean, I go all out every year for Christmas. I bought you a MacBook last year."

"Last year you were still living with our parents and not paying any bills. You're a full-fledged adult now. You can't blow money like this."

"Fine!" Lola throws her arms up in defeat. "We'll look at the clearance racks."

"That's not what I meant--" His sister covers her ears as she makes her way to the clearance section. "Okay, fine," he groans. "I'm giving you a $25 limit on the shirt."

Lola spends ten minutes looking at each shirt on the tiny rack before finally settling on a gorgeous soft blue button-up. "This color would look so good on him." She smiles at the thought of her husband wearing the soft shirt she picked out for him at Christmas dinner. "Don't you think?"

"Absolutely. Now let's go. They close in fifteen minutes." Tyler grabs her hand and pulls her to the checkout line before she can find anything else.

"Thanks for coming with me today," she says once they're in Tyler's car and driving away from the mall.

"Please don't ever stress me out like this two days before a major holiday ever again." Her brother begs and grabs some aspirin from Lola's glove compartment and downs it.

"Don't be dramatic." Lola rolls her eyes and turns the radio on to the only local station playing Christmas music. "Don't judge me, but I'm kind of nervous."

Tyler's bushy eyebrows pull together. "What are you nervous about?"

"Christmas," Lola admits.

Looking ahead, he blinks several times. "I don't understand."

"You'll get it when you're married."

"No, I'm pretty sure I won't. Josh has already married you. He agreed to spend the rest of his life with you. What is there to be nervous about?"

"I'm worried he won't like what I got for him." She admits, looking ahead.

"No offense, but you make me want to bash my head against the steering wheel. You're putting way too much importance on one day. You know Josh. He's not the type of guy to let a Christmas gift sway his real feelings for you."

"I know that. And I know I'm being irrational... he just didn't get a lot of Christmases growing up. His family was too dysfunctional to celebrate. I just want it to be special. You, mom, and dad are all going to see Terry in Alaska so it's just going to be us. I just... want him to know I'm always going to be there for him." Tyler's face softens as he looks over at his sister.

"Lola, he knows that. You know that he knows that." Lola slows the car to a stop in front of her parents' house. "Hey, don't worry. It's gonna be great." Tyler reaches over and pats his sisters' arm. "I'll see you after the holidays. Love you."

"I love you, too. Have fun and tell Terry I love her."

"Of course," Tyler promised and leaned over the center console to hug his sister. Without another word he gets out of the car and pulls his collar up to protect his neck from the cold winter evening. "See you in a week!"

"Bye!" Lola calls after him and watches to make sure he makes it into the house safely. Once he's inside, she reverses out of the driveway and begins the drive home. When she walks into the third floor apartment, she immediately hides the bag behind her back as her six-foot husband makes his way to greet her at the door.

"Hey! How was Tyler?" He asks and leans down to give her a quick kiss on her cheek before making his way back to the kitchen.

"He was great!" She smiles and rushes back to their shared room. "He got the last-minute gift he was looking for, and I found you something else." She shoves the bag into the closet to hide it from Josh.

"Lola, you don't have to give me anything. You especially didn't have to get me five gifts. It's too much." He follows her into the room and grabs her waist as she turns to face him. "Seriously, it'll just be perfect with just us two. I don't need anything." She looks up into her husband's hazel eyes and smiles.

"I know, but you're getting gifts whether you like it or not, mister." She pats his toned chest and walks out of the room.

"You know we could have used that money for a small trip out of town."

"We can do that for our anniversary. What's for dinner? It smells amazing!" Lola quickly changes the subject as she walks into their small kitchen.

"I made chili in the slow cooker, I hope you like it." He reaches into the cabinets and grabs two bowls.

"I love your chili." Lola smiles and takes a bowl from him. "Thank you for cooking," She steps up on her tiptoes to kiss his cheek.

"It's the least I could do since I was home all day." Josh smiles and leans into her kiss. "So, I was thinking tomorrow after we take your family to the airport, we'll come back here and watch some Christmas movies, drink hot cocoa and just... relax."

"Just relax, huh?" She waggles her eyebrows playfully.

"Pervert," He playfully smacks his wife on her butt.

"I'd love that. But alas; there will be no relaxing." Lola scoops herself a bowl of chili and walks over to the fridge. "I've gotta wrap the last of your presents and we're watching Leah's boys for her while she finishes getting the house ready for Christmas before she works tomorrow."

"Right, right. The twins. What about Carly?"

"She has to work as well."

"Well, it sounds like we better enjoy our alone time." Josh reaches around his small wife to grab the sour cream and cheese.

"After her sister comes to get them, then we can... 'relax' all we want." She walks over to the table and takes a seat, ready to enjoy her dinner.

"We could just 'relax' right now." Josh sets his bowl down and grabs his wife's hand.

"But... my chili." She pouts but continues to follow him to their bedroom.

~~*~~

Lola can't sleep. She finally gets out of bed at six that morning after tossing and turning all night and makes her way to the living room to wait for Josh to wake up. Finally, Christmas has arrived. She can't wait to see the look on Josh's face when he finally opens all his gifts. He'll know just how much she truly loves him and is grateful to have him in water.

She hopes that making them breakfast would pass the time, but it only makes her more anxious as she waits for Josh to wake up. She finally gives up and walks into the bedroom and sits on the edge of the bed. "Josh," She nudges her husband to try and wake him. "Babe, it's Christmas. I made breakfast." She pokes Josh's side. "Come on, I've been up for an *hour*."

"Ten more minutes." Josh groans and covers his head with the covers.

"Absolutely not. Get. Up." She stands up and grabs Josh's arm to pull him out of bed. "I made French toast and *everything*."

"That's all you had to say," Josh says with a new sense of energy. "Come on, Lola!" He sits up and they dash into the dining area to eat their breakfast. "This is delicious," Josh says through a mouth full of food. "I didn't know you could cook."

Lola gasps as her eyes widen. "I cook for you at least twice a week."

Guilty he grins. "About that…"

"Are you serious?!" She squeals while swatting his arm.

With a playful chuckle, he pulls away. "I love you."

"If you truly loved me, you wouldn't think my cooking is bad," she grumbles. She's not really upset despite the pout on her face. Truthfully she knows that she's not the best cook. That's why Josh provides dinner most nights. That's also another reason why she's so desperate to make this Christmas perfect. She feels like he drew the short straw when it comes to wives. She's not a great cook. She doesn't keep their home immaculately clean. And most days she can't be bothered to put on makeup. The least she can do is show him how much she loves him by showering him with gifts.

After they finish eating breakfast and clean their dishes, Lola excitedly grabs her husband's hand and pulls him to the light brown sofa in their living room.

"Have a seat," she orders while simultaneously pushing him down.

He chuckles. "Ooh, are we about to have some fun?"

"Not that kind of fun you pervert," she laughs. She turns to the Christmas tree and grabs the stack of gifts with his name labeled on them. "Open them," she encourages with a large grin.

Josh's mouth turns up. "Maybe you should open your presents first."

"No way. I'm too excited to see your reaction."

"Alright, here it goes." He grabs the smallest of the gifts and rips off the wrapping paper revealing a disposable jewelry box. Inside of the box is a nice silver watch that he knows must have cost at least $100. "Oh wow, thanks, babe."

"Do you like it?" Lola asks with a bright grin.

"I do," he murmurs while clasping the watch around his wrist. The next gift is a pair of wireless headphones. They're even more expensive than the watch.

"I know how much you've wanted those."

"Um, yeah." Josh clears his throat as he opens the third gift. It's a new laptop. "What?"

"You needed one," Lola giggles.

Slowly he shakes his head. "I barely use the one I already have. You shouldn't have bought this."

She pouts. "Do you not like it?"

"I do like it, but I don't need it." He sighs as he lifts the fourth box. Luckily all he finds inside is a pair of dark pants. "These aren't my usual style but they're nice."

"There's one more gift," Lola reminds him.

"You really went all out this year," he stiffly chuckles while opening the final gift. Inside is a pale blue button shirt with a white lion head embroidered on chest pocket.

"Do you like it?" She excitedly demands.

"Um, I already have it."

"What?" Her mouth pops open. "No. No way."

"I'm sorry sweetie. Mom bought this for me last year."

Lola groans and throws back her head. "I'm such an idiot. I've ruined Christmas."

He stares at her with furrowed eyebrows. "What?"

"You should divorce me. I'm such a screw-up."

He's baffled by her reaction. "Over a shirt?"

"It's not about the shirt. It's about me ruining our special moments. This is our first Christmas as a married couple. I wanted it to be perfect. Instead, I bought you a laptop that you don't want and a shirt that you already have. I'm so stupid."

Quickly he sets aside the shirt and lifts his hands. "Whoa, whoa, babe you've got to calm down."

"Tyler told me I was doing too much, and he was right. You hate everything, don't you? How could I have been so stupid--"

"Lola, stop!" Josh grabs her hands and holds them to his chest. "You're not a screw-up, and you're not stupid. Don't you ever talk about yourself like that ever again. I don't hate the gifts."

"I just wanted everything to be perfect." Lola pouts and folds her arms over her chest.

"It *is* perfect."

"No, it's not," she says adamantly.

"Yes, it is! Not because of the gifts or the breakfast. But because we're spending it together. That's more than I could have possibly ever asked for. I love you, and no matter what you did or didn't do for me, today would have been perfect."

"You're gonna make me cry." Lola sticks out her bottom lip.

"Don't cry, *mi amor*." Josh cradles her face in one of his hands. "Thank you. I appreciate everything you got for me."

"I kept the receipts in case you didn't like them."

He sighs with relief. "Oh thank God. All of that junk is going back." Lola reaches out and playfully smacks his arm. "Okay, okay. Maybe just the laptop. I'm keeping the watch."

"And the headphones?"

"And the headphones." He leans over and kisses his wife softly. "Okay, your turn!" Eagerly he hands her the gifts with a smile on his face. He knows how desperate she was to make today perfect for him, but all he wanted for Christmas was for her to wake up beside him for the rest of their lives.

'Tis The Season

Another day, another post on social media of one of Samantha's high school classmates getting engaged. Would the day ever come for her? She was beginning to lose hope. Her boyfriend of six years shows no signs that he's even thinking about proposing. He says they're basically married because they live together and do all the things that married couples do. Well, except for one thing. Heath doesn't want to have children until they're married. The only problem is Samantha doesn't think they'll ever be married. She loves him, but she's not getting any younger. Her thirtieth birthday is less than a year away and all she has to show for her life is a successful career as a pediatrician. It's not easy treating innocent little ones day in and day out while wondering if you'll ever have one. Especially when you know the only reason you don't have one is because your boyfriend has no interest in being a husband.

Or at least that's what she thinks. In actuality, Heath has been planning the perfect proposal for over a year. He has the ring, the location, and the song. All that's missing is the day. He knows what day he wants to enact his plan, but the problem is he's not sure Samantha will remain patient until Christmas morning. He's not a fool. He can see how she's pulling away. It's his own fault. Watching his parents' marriage publicly implode deterred him from wanting to enter such an arrangement. Now he may not get the chance to ask the woman he loves to spend the rest of her life with him. He really can't blame her for her obvious frustration. If the shoe was on the other foot, he would probably feel the same way. He just hopes he can make it right before she tries to walk away.

"I don't know, Nicki," Samantha complains to her best friend over the phone as she cleans up the living room of the house she and Heath share. "I feel like if it's not tonight, I gotta walk."

"Think about this rationally," Nicki starts. "Heath loves you. He comes from a broken home. His parents went through a really rough divorce. You knew going into this that he'd probably wait a while to propose. Look at Josh! The man finally proposed to Lola after five and a half years."

"Lola's a lot more patient than I am, apparently. And it's been six years. The frustrating part is that we've *talked* about getting married multiple times throughout the years, and every time I think it's going to happen it just... doesn't."

"I think it's coming. It'll probably happen a lot sooner than you think. You just gotta wait it out."

"I really don't think I can, Nicki." An alarm goes off in Samantha's ear and she drops the last of the decorative pillows onto the couch. "Shoot, I gotta go. I'm gonna be late for work."

"It's Christmas Eve, though!"

"There are still sick kids." Samantha hangs up and rushes out the door to try to get to work in time. "Bye, Heath! Love you!" She calls back as she shuts the front door behind her.

Heath sticks his head out of the bedroom door to make sure his long-term girlfriend actually left before dialing her best friend. "Hey, does she suspect anything?" He asks as soon as Nicki answers the phone.

"She's got one foot out the door, Heath. I'm telling you, you have to do it tonight or she's going to be gone."

"What?! No, it *has* to be tomorrow. Christmas is her favorite holiday. I have everything planned out--"

"Heath. Listen to me. She's leaving if you don't do it soon." Heath ran a hand through his shaggy brown hair. "She loves you, don't let me make you think she doesn't. She wants to spend her life with you, but she's starting to feel like it's just not going to happen. She wants kids, and you don't want kids until you're married. But you told her last year you don't think you want to get married… and you had a *ring* for her already."

"I had to throw her off my trail!" Heath defends himself as he scrambles to his bedside table where he has the ring carefully hidden in the back of the drawer. He checks it twice a day to make sure it's still there. His anxiety has gotten the best of him and he's been terrified of losing it since the day he paid it off.

"Yeah, and by throwing her off your trail, you basically pushed her out the door," Nicki explained. "Can you please just trust me on this? You love her, right?"

"Of course!"

"Propose tonight." Nicki hangs up before Heath has a chance to argue again.

Heath paces the bedroom floor. Would she really leave him if he doesn't propose *tonight*? He decides to stick with his original plan. She wouldn't leave him on Christmas Eve. He'll be fine to propose in the morning.

~~*~~

Samantha comes home after a long day and kicks off her shoes. "Heath? Are you home?" She calls out as she makes her way to the bedroom. "Hello?" No reply. She takes a deep breath and looks over the room. Can she really walk out on him? Can she leave him after all they've been through together? "Okay," she tells herself. "If he's not home in the next ten minutes… I leave." She closes her eyes and prays that he shows up in time.

The next fifteen minutes pass by slowly. She even gives him an extra five minutes to come home. Unfortunately, he doesn't make it. With a heavy heart, she pushes herself up off the couch and goes back to the room to start gathering her things. She doesn't have much since she and Heath share most of the items in their home. It's been that way ever since they moved in together four years ago after she completed medical school.

All her clothes fit into a suitcase. Her personal electronics are already in her car, so she's ready to go. The problem is, she doesn't want to. She doesn't want to walk out of the door and leave behind her life with Heath. Despite the slow pace, he's kept their relationship at, they've had a lot of good times. She loves him, and she's pretty sure that he loves her.

"Come on. Please come home." She silently begs and stares at the door, willing Heath to open it and walk in at any given moment. It doesn't happen. "Alright, I guess there's no point delaying any further." As she reaches the door, it yanks open and Heath is standing there with a ham.

"Hey! You're home." He kisses her cheek. "You wouldn't believe how insane the stores were today. And I couldn't find a ham that was big enough to feed everyone tomorrow." He continues to talk as he walks to the kitchen. "So I had to stop by my mom's house, and you know how that is. Thankfully she had a ham we could use for tomorrow. She says hello, by the way. She won't be able to make it tomorrow since Dad's coming. Something about not wanting to ruin Christmas dinner by stabbing him in the eye with a butter knife and--hey, why do you have a bag packed?"

"I can't do this anymore," she says with a heavy sigh. Her voice is thick with emotion. "I'm sorry. I just can't wait on you to finally decide when you're ready to settle down. I know you need time and your family is a mess, but I'm ready, and I don't think you'll be ready any time soon."

His eyes widen as he sets the large brown paper bag on the countertop. "What are you talking about? I am settled down. We are settled down."

"You know that's not what I mean," Samantha scoffs and shuts the front door. "I want to start a family with you, and you're not wanting to do that until we're married. But I don't think you're ever planning to marry me. It's not fair. I don't have many years of fertility left. I need to find someone who is ready and willing to have the things in life that I want to have."

His head shakes. "Samantha, please..."

"No, it's okay. Really." Samantha sighs and adjusts the bag on her shoulder. "It's not fair to either of us to continue like this. I feel like I'm always going to be waiting on you, and it's not fair for me to push you into something you don't want. Something has to give, so I'm taking one for the team. This is the end. We're done."

"But, I love you and you love me."

She shrugs, "Sometimes love isn't enough."

"This isn't what I wanted," Heath mutters and paces the living room.

"You think this is what I wanted to have to do? Do you think this isn't breaking my heart? Heath... you told me last year you didn't think you were ever wanting to get married and I still stayed. It hurt like hell to hear you say that, but I still stayed."

"I didn't mean that."

"Then why did you say it?" She demands with a scowl on her face.

"Please, let's just go to bed. We can figure this out in the morning. We can sleep on it. If you still want to leave, then I won't stop you. No matter how much it breaks my heart." His voice is filled with emotion.

A tear rolls down her cheek. "If I don't leave now, I never will."

Desperately he reaches for her. She steps back before his hands can touch her skin. "Would that really be such a bad thing?"

She sobs, "Heath--" It's too hard for her to say the words that she knows she needs to say. It's too hard to accept that this is the end of them.

"Fine. Fine, if you want to leave, I'm not going to stop you just... wait here. You should at least have your Christmas gift."

"No, please don't make this harder than it has to be," she practically begs.

"I've had this one picked out for you for over a year. Just... please." He expels a breath and looks at the ceiling. "Let me give it to you." Before she can refuse, Heath runs to their room. He sees how empty she's left it. The drawers of the dresser she claimed for herself long ago are pulled out with nothing inside of them. Her half of the open closet is bare. Even her cell phone charger has been removed from the outlet on her side of the bed. Taking a deep breath, he grabs the ring out of the bedside table and brings it out to the woman he still holds a flicker of hope for.

"What is this?"

"It's what you wanted most. I have everything planned out for tomorrow morning because I know how much you like cheesy Christmas romance stories, so I wanted to give you one of your own," he explains and clears his throat, trying to hold back the emotion. "I have a song picked out. 'I'll Be Home For Christmas'. I have a sign in the back of the closet behind my suits, asking you to marry me."

"What?" Samantha's breath catches in her throat.

"I was going to make you breakfast and put on The Santa Clause and ask you to marry me. I love you. Correction, I am in love with you. You are the only woman I notice in this world. I want you to have everything you want and more. It's what you deserve, and I'm sorry. I'm so sorry it took me so long to be ready, but I've been ready for almost a year. I just wanted to make it perfect because that's what you deserve. It's what you've always deserved, especially after putting up with my bullshit for as long as you have. I'm an idiot for not doing this sooner."

"If this is some trick to get me to stay--"

"It's not. You can even call Nicki and ask her. She's been helping me plan everything."

"Oh my gosh, that's why she told me to be patient."

"She told me to do it sooner. She's been telling me for weeks and I just didn't listen to her. I wanted to do this on Christmas. I wanted this year to be extra special for you and I screwed it up--"

"Yes."

"Yes, I screwed up. Is that what you mean?" She shakes her head. "Wait... Are you saying yes you'll marry me?"

"Yes, I'm saying I'll marry you, Heath. I will spend the rest of my life with you idiotic, clueless, wonderful man because I love you. You're the only man I notice in this world."

He runs up to Samantha and wraps her in his arms, lifting her into the air. "Oh, my God I really thought that would end differently."

She giggles, "You thought I would say no."

"Well, shit, yeah. You were already one foot out the door in the most literal sense."

"Then why did you ask?"

"Desperate times call for desperate measures." He sets her down and grabs her left hand, slipping the delicate diamond ring on her finger. "I love you."

"I love you, too." She stretches her neck to press her lips against his as her alarm goes off, signaling the strike of midnight. "Merry Christmas."

"Merry Christmas." Heath leans down and kisses his fiancée.

Samantha looks at the sparkling ring on her hand. "I can't believe we're engaged."

He kisses her again before verbally responding. "'Tis the season."

The Happy Family

Stefanie sighs as she looks at the pictures of happy families on her Facebook feed. They look perfect with their coordinating outfits and bright smiles. She wishes she could know what that is like just once in her life. There's one family from two towns over in Golden Shore, Virginia that has spent the last few weeks with her, but she doubts they're interested in adopting her. That's how it's been her whole life. Every time a family shows a little interest and she gets her hopes up, they choose to bring a younger child into their families instead. It's happened enough times that she should be used to it, but she's still disappointed every time.

"Stefanie! Lights out in five!" Ms. Linda, the woman in charge of the group home she lives in, calls up the stairs. There are six other girls residing in the four-bedroom house. Stefanie shares a room with one other girl. They're the oldest two in the house which should bond them, but it does the opposite. Unlike Stefanie, Ashley has given up hope of ever being adopted. She has made it known on more than one occasion that she thinks Stefanie is foolish for still wanting it to happen.

With a heavy sigh, Stefanie locks her cell phone and sets it aside on the nightstand. There's only two days until Christmas, and her hopes of being adopted before then are proving to be fruitless. The Miller family are nice people, but sometimes it feels like they're trying too hard to make her like them. Truthfully, she has enjoyed spending time with them over the past weeks. She has never really liked any of the families that have shown an interest in her in the past. Perhaps because she could sense that their interest wouldn't last long. The Millers are different. They're genuinely interested in getting to know her.

Or at least that's what she thought before. It's the day the Millers promised to come back to see Stefanie. It's time for lights out, but there's been no sign of the Miller family. Maybe Ashely is right. Maybe it's foolish of her to think hopeful parents-to-be would be interested in making her their daughter. After all, she's already 16. What family in their right mind would want to adopt a 16-year-old? She only has a little over a year before she'll be kicked out of the foster system. She has no idea what she'll do on her own. Where will she live? How will she pay her bills?

"I told you not to get your hopes up," Ashley says with a smirk on her round face as she walks into the room. She likes to be right even when it hurts someone's feelings.

"Not right now, Ashley. I'm not in the mood," Stefanie mumbles and turns away from the girl.

"I bet getting your hopes up then having them crushed is mood dampening." Stefanie rolls her eyes but doesn't verbally respond. That doesn't deter Ashley. "Isn't the couple young? There's no way you could have honestly believed that they would want to adopt you. People like that don't want a kid that's older than four."

Heavily, Stefanie sighs. "You've made your point. Can we please go to sleep now?"

Ashley shrugs her shoulders. "Sure. I've said everything I need to say. It's nice to see you stepping into reality. It's been a long time coming."

That night Stefanie tries her hardest to get some sleep. It's hard to do with all of the thoughts swirling around her mind. She really believed that the Millers would be her family. Ashley's right, they are a young couple. Liam is a recent medical school graduate and his wife, Jennifer, owns a clothing shop. They have a golden retriever named Lucky that they've brought around for Stefanie to meet. Foolishly she took that as a sign that they wanted the dog to get familiar with so that when she inevitably moved into their home, Lucky wouldn't freak out. She was wrong. The Millers don't want her. They've probably already taken their newborn child home. While she's not surprised, she's more than disappointed this time around. She's heartbroken. She truly allowed herself to get close to Liam and Jennifer. She allowed herself to imagine a life with them. It would have been a happy one.

As she falls asleep, she hopes they'll show up tomorrow and bring her home for Christmas. She knows it's a naive wish to me, but she can't help it. She doesn't easily get her hopes up. She doesn't know how to just let it go.

~~*~~

Stefanie doesn't want to get out of bed the next day. She pulls the cover over her head, blocking out the bright winter sunshine. She's too sad to socialize with anyone.

"This is pathetic," Ashley scoffs as she comes back into their shared room near noon. "You've been in bed all day. Ms. Linda is very annoyed with your behavior."

"I don't care," Stefanie grumbles. Her voice is thick with emotion.

"Have you even showered today?"

"I'll shower when I'm ready."

"This is insane. You knew not to get your hopes up..." Before Ashely can continue her rant, Stefanie reaches into her bedside table and pulls out her headphones. She's not in the mood to argue this Christmas Eve, especially not with a cynic like Ashley. "Oh, real mature." She hears before sticking the small buds in her ears and pushing play on her "Sad Bitch Hours" playlist. She just wants to be left alone for a few hours.

Stefanie doesn't know how long she lays in her bed listening to depressing music. The sun is long gone from the sky and Ashley hasn't come back to their room. She rolls onto her side in the twin-sized bed. Her cell phone's battery is dying. Reluctantly she stops the music and throws the comforter off her body. She can at least shower before she goes downstairs in search of something to eat.

The hot water and steam help to clear away the funk she's in. She even brushes her teeth and hair. After dressing in fuzzy Christmas pajamas that some church group donated to the group home, Stefanie walks down the wooden staircase. The living room is filled with the other residents of the house. They gathered around the old TV watching *the Grinch*. She doesn't bother saying anything to them. Instead, she turns to the left and walks through the dining room to the kitchen. Ms. Linda is leaning against the counter studying a cookbook. The older woman isn't terrible to live with. She keeps all of the girls well-fed and tries to make the group home feel like a family. She's also paid by the state to do it, so Stefanie is always wary of how genuine the woman's intentions may be.

"Well hey, Stef. How are you feeling?" Ms. Linda asks as she sets the timer on the oven. "Ashely said you had an upset stomach?"

"Yeah, something like that." Stefanie sighs and makes her way over to the cabinets to find something quick to eat. "I'm feeling a little better now, though."

"I hope it's not contagious. The last time this house came down with an illness, I didn't sleep for a week."

"I remember," Stefanie gives a small laugh and continues her search. "Is it okay if I just make a can of soup and go back to bed?"

"Of course. Get all the rest you need." Ms. Linda gives her a soft smile and turns back to the stove. She's been there every time Stefanie has had an adoption fall through or a family changed their mind at the last minute. Stefanie doubts that Ms. Linda believes she really has an upset stomach, but the woman goes along with it to not upset her any further.

"Thank you, Ms. Linda. I really appreciate everything you do for us."

"You don't have to thank me, honey." The woman waves away her words. When she acts that way, it makes Stefanie wonder if the woman truly does care about them despite being paid to be their caretaker. It makes Stefanie think that there's someone out there who can love her and want to be a part of her life. Maybe. Hopefully.

A knock at the door pulls Stefanie from her thoughts as she grabs a can of chicken noodle soup from one of the cabinets. She doesn't bother to respond to it. It's probably another donation or something of the sort.

"Ashley, please answer the door," Ms. Linda calls out.

"I can't. This movie is really good."

Ms. Linda rolls her eyes. "You know, she's watched that movie a thousand times, but whatever." She nudges Stefanie as she passes by. "Can you watch that on the stove? It shouldn't be too much longer." Stefanie nods and puts her soup on to cook as well. She can barely hear voices in the foyer. "Stefanie, come here please," Ms. Linda calls to her.

Stefanie rolls her eyes but walks out of the kitchen. Her eyes are focused on her feet as she walks. She hates when they have to say thank you for the donations they receive. It's always awkward. People seem to only do it just to say they did something selfless during the holiday season.

"Look who's here, honey." Ms. Linda's voice is light with expectation as she waits for Stefanie to lift her head and look at the newest arrivals.

Stefanie's eyes widen as she stares at the young couple. "Liam, Jennifer, what are you doing here?"

"We're here for you," Jennifer laughs as she steps forward and pulls the girl into a hug. "I'm so sorry we didn't come yesterday. We got held up with something rather important."

Stefanie gulps, this must be the moment they'll tell her that they've chosen another kid. "It's okay. I understand."

Liam chuckles, "You're a smart girl. So, what are you waiting for? Go get your stuff."

"Wait. What." Stefanie blinks a few times, trying to understand what she's hearing. "Get my stuff?"

"The adoption agency finally approved our request this afternoon. We wanted to come and bring you home earlier, but we wanted to make sure your room was ready." Jennifer explains, trying to hold back her emotions. "Liam said we should wait until Christmas, but I told him that you've waited long enough."

Stefanie blinks again and again. "I'm... wait you're bringing me with you?"

Liam smiles fondly at her. "Of course, honey. You're our daughter. We've known from the first time we met you that we wanted to bring you home with us. Now we finally get to do it."

"What are you waiting for? Go get your things," Ms. Linda encourages. "It's a good thing your stomach stopped hurting, right?"

Jennifer gasps and carefully grips Stefanie's arms as she studies her face. "Are you sick?"

"Not anymore," Stefanie answers with a shake of her head. "I'll, um, go get my things now."

"I'll help," one of the younger girls volunteers. Giddily, Stefanie runs up the stairs with the girl, Haley, beside her. "This is so exciting! How do you feel?" Haley asks as Stefanie grabs her small suitcase and opens it on her bed.

"Honestly, I can't believe this is happening."

"Me either," Ashley scoffs while leaning against the door jamb. Her eyes are narrowed with a glare.

"Aw Ashley, aren't you happy for Stefanie?"

"No, why should I be? Why is getting adopted when we're all still stuck here? Is it because she's a blonde-haired, blue-eyed, American favorite?"

"Ashley, you have blonde hair too," Haley comments jokingly.

Ashley pushes away from the door jamb and stomps into the bedroom. "Don't get too comfortable with your new mommy and daddy. They'll ship you back here as soon as the holidays are over."

"No, they won't," Stefanie vehemently denies. "Maybe if you change your attitude a family would show more interest in you. You're always pushing people away."

"I'm not like you. I don't need anyone."

"It's sad that you think that."

Haley frowns. "Stefanie, you should probably change. It's cold outside."

"You're right. I'll be down in a second to say goodbye to everyone." Stefanie shoos her foster sisters out of the room so she can change into her favorite sweater and a pair of faded blue jeans.

She doesn't have much, so she packs the last of her things into her small suitcase, including the friendship bracelet that she and Ashley made when they first moved into the group house nearly six years ago. Carefully she looks around her old room to make sure she has all of her belongings. Once she's certain, she drags her suitcase down the stairs and says goodbye to Ms. Linda and all her foster sisters, even Ashley who is still scowling.

"I'll make sure no one tries to take your bed," the girl grumbles.

Ms. Linda shakes her head. "Be nice, Ashley. You're going to miss Stefanie."

Ashley scoffs, "Not likely."

The drive to her new home is longer than she anticipated. The foster home is a few towns over, so she ends up falling asleep in the backseat mid-conversation with her new parents. When they get to their small home in Golden Shore, they gently wake Stefanie up and guide her to her new room. She's half-asleep so she doesn't quite get to take in her new home before practically falling onto the memory foam mattress of her queen-sized bed.

Jennifer covers her new daughter with the duvet and plugs her phone in for her. "Do you think she'll like it here?" She asks Liam as she exits the room, shutting the door behind her.

"Did you see how happy she was when we came to get her? She's going to love it, Jen." He kisses his wife's forehead. "Come on, let's put her stuff under the tree."

~~*~~

It's early when Stefanie wakes on Christmas morning. The sunlight streams through the transparent lavender curtains on her windows. She sits up in the bed and looks around the room. There's a white bookshelf to the right of the windows with a quilted sofa in front of the windows. There aren't a lot of books on the shelves, but there is a framed picture of her with Jennifer and Liam from the third time they spent time together. The white vanity dresser matches the farmhouse-style bed and nightstand. A mirror hangs on the back of a door she assumes leads to a closet. She decides to unpack her suitcase. When she opens her closet, she's surprised to find despite it being a walk-in, it's almost halfway full with clothes.

There's a soft knock on her bedroom door as Jennifer walks into the room. "You're awake. How did you sleep?"

"Great. That bed is the softest thing I've ever laid on."

"I'm glad you like it. Are you hungry?"

Stefanie nods her head. "I could eat."

"Okay, let's go eat breakfast." She steps into the hallway and motions for Stefanie to follow her. They walk along the carpeted floor eventually stepping into a rectangular foyer that's furnished with a chrome and glass console table and a couple of standing lamps. Jennifer turns to the entrance on the right where the kitchen is. There's a rectangular dining table with six chairs in front of the bay window. The counters, cabinets, and appliances are all much nicer than those in the group house.

Liam is standing at the cooking range on the island frying eggs. "Good morning, sleepyhead. You're just in time for breakfast. Do you like fried eggs?"

Stefanie nods, "I do."

"What about hash browns?"

"I like those too."

"And buttermilk biscuits?"

"I don't have any complaints."

"Good. We'll get along just fine," he jokes.

Jennifer opens the refrigerator and pulls out various juices. "Which do you want, Stefanie?"

"Oh, um, I can pour my own if that's alright."

"That's perfectly fine. The drinking glasses are in the cabinet to the right of the microwave." Jennifer motions to the designated cabinet.

Stefanie hesitates. "Is this real?"

"What do you mean?" Jennifer asks her.

"Am I really going to stay with you? This isn't just for Christmas, right?"

"What? Of course it's real," Liam takes the pan off the flame and sits next to Stefanie. "Stefanie, we wanted to bring you home with us the moment we met you. We knew you were our daughter. Why would you think this is just for Christmas?"

"I don't know… just something Ashely said, I guess. She kind of got in my head." Stefanie admits. "I've wanted this for so long, and now that it's happened it feels like it's not going to last."

"Oh, honey," Jennifer sits on her other side. "We're not going to leave you. Like it or not, you're stuck with us."

"You know I'll be eighteen in two years, right?"

Liam shrugs his shoulders as he distributes the food onto plates. "You'll still be our daughter."

"You'll still have a home with us. Even if you're around until you're thirty, this is your home," Jennifer explains. Lucky barrels into the kitchen smelling the food. "Now let's eat before the dog steals everything. We have a busy day ahead of us."

Jennifer isn't kidding when she says they have a busy day ahead. During breakfast, Liam announces that they're hosting Christmas dinner for the extended family. The announcement makes Stefanie nervous, but she doesn't have time to dwell on it. Her new parents lead her to the Christmas tree in the cozy living room where several gifts are wrapped and placed beneath it. Jennifer grabs one of the boxes and hands it to her.

"Oh, you got me a gift."

Liam chuckles and shakes his head. "We got you several gifts."

Stefanie's eyes widen. "You didn't have to do that." She isn't used to getting more than one present on Christmas.

"We wanted to."

They watch with happy smiles as Stefanie opens each gift one by one. They bought her clothes, shoes, and even a new iPad that they claim is meant to help her with her schoolwork. When she's done unwrapping her presents, Jennifer walks with her back to her bedroom to help her find something to wear. Together they choose a rich red dress with quarter sleeves and a loose skirt. Stefanie has never worn anything so nice. She's excited when she sees it matches Jennifer's sweater dress and Liam's necktie.

"Can we take a picture in front of the tree before the night is over?"

"Of course," the couple happily agrees.

Stefanie helps Jennifer and Liam cook dinner. She's not sure what to do, but they don't seem to mind having her in the kitchen. Preparing the food and setting the table helps keep her mind off of the arrival of her new family. Soon enough the doorbell rings.

"Stefanie, I want you to meet my parents, Tina and Patrick," Jennifer introduces.

"Hi, it's nice to meet you," Stefanie says quietly.

Liam's parents arrive next along with his sister, brother-in-law, and their daughter. They all sit around the table laughing and talking with ease. No one is bothered by Stefanie's presence. If anything, it's almost like they are expecting her to be here.

"Since we're all here," Liam starts and the room goes quiet. "I just want to thank you all for supporting us on our adoption journey. We didn't think we'd get approved as quickly as we did, and it's all thanks to everyone's kind words about us and your prayers. We couldn't be happier to have Stefanie in our family. That being said, dinner is served! Thank you all for being here." Conversation broke out as the family members made their way to fill their plates with all the delicious foods Liam and Jennifer made.

Stefanie stays back and watches as her new family fills the house with laughter and conversation. She can't help but get teary-eyed as she realizes how lucky she is to be a part of this happy family.

Home for the Holidays

"I'm finally home," Georgia sighs as she parks in the driveway of the ranch-style two-story house she grew up in. She hasn't visited her small town since she graduated from college six years ago. Not because she has anything against her home. Her family has merely made it a habit to spend the holidays at different locations. Last year they celebrated Christmas in Milan. The year before that she took a cruise to the Bahamas. With the announcement of her sister's pregnancy, Georgia's parents decided it's best to celebrate at home. It'll be like old times with her and her siblings staying in the house with their parents. She's actually excited for the next week.

As she approaches the front door, it swings open revealing a woman with caramel skin, dark hair in kinky curls, and a swollen belly. The woman grabs Georgia in an excited hug.

"I didn't think you were coming."

"Why on earth wouldn't I come, Lana?"

Lana shrugs her shoulders. "I don't know. You're a big city woman now."

Georgia laughs and walks into the warm house. "Yeah, but I came from a small town." She rolls her suitcase to the wooden staircase. "Is Chad here, yet?"

"Yes, but he, Dad, and Mark went out somewhere." Mark is Lana's husband. He and Chad went to college together which is how Mark and Lana met. Chad and Lana are twins. They went to the same college and stayed in dorms that were only five minutes away from each other. After they graduated, Lana moved back to Golden Shore while Mark went off to medical school in New York with his cousin, Liam. Chad still lives in NYC, but Lana is happily married and settled in their hometown. She never stops trying to convince Georgia to move back and embrace the simple life.

"I'll help you unpack," Lana volunteers as they enter Georgia's childhood bedroom. Not much has changed besides the covers on the full-sized bed and the lack of boy band posters on the walls.

"You are way too happy to have me around."

"I'm hoping that you'll love being home so much that you'll decide to stay."

Georgia snorts, "That's doubtful." Her chocolate-colored hand swipes the kinky curly front of her hair off of her forehead. "Although, I am happy to spend a week in Golden Shore. Do they still host the Christmas festival in the park?" The town's park is a circular stretch of lawn in the middle of the area where nearly every business is. There's a large gazebo and a small playground for children. Growing up, every year from six o'clock to nine o'clock, Golden Shore would host a Christmas festival in the park. There would be hot cocoa, candy canes, caroling, and a gift raffle.

"Yep. It's a small town. We don't welcome change here."

Georgia giggles as she closes the top drawer of her chest of drawers. "You're right about that." As she speaks a thud sounds from the distance. Her eyebrows furrow. "What was that?"

Lana claps her hands excitedly. "That is my favorite part of the day." She walks to the window overlooking the backyard and waves her sister forward.

"What is going on?"

"Just come look," Lana urges. Curiously, Georgia joins her at the window. Lana points to their neighbor's yard. There's a man with golden corded arms being showcased in his short-sleeved shirt chopping wood. "Our very own piece of eye candy in little old Golden Shore."

"Who is that?" Georgia asks.

"That is Declan Theodore."

"I didn't know he was home." Georgia faintly recalls the boy who lived next door. He's three years younger than the twins, but a year older than her. She didn't really get to know him until her siblings went to college. Their strange friendship started with him offering her a ride to school. Then she started watching his baseball practices. They got close, so close that people thought they were dating. Georgia thought maybe they would, but just two days before he graduated, Declan announced that he had enlisted in the Navy. They lost touch after he completed basic training and was stationed on a base in California.

"He came back about a month ago. Cheryl was so happy to have her only son home that she was yelling about it all over town."

"Is he on leave or something?"

"No, he's back for good according to Cheryl. He's staying in an apartment above their garage for now."

"He looks ... different."

Lana laughs and turns away from the window. "He looks good." Georgia gapes at her sister. She shrugs her shoulders. "What? I may be married but I can still look."

Georgia steals one more glance at Declan before walking away from the window. "Well, it's good he's back, I guess."

"Mm-hmm. Are you going to talk to him? I'm sure he'll be happy to see you again."

"Um, I don't know. We haven't talked in a decade."

Again Lana shrugs her shoulders. "That doesn't matter."

"Actually, I think it does," Georgia comments. She gathers her hair and pulls it into a ponytail. The drive from Atlanta to Golden Shore took over eight hours. She's tired and in desperate need of food. "Is Ralph's still open? I'm craving a bowl of spaghetti and chili."

"Ralph's will never go out of business. It's the most affordable place to eat if you don't feel like cooking, especially now that that overpriced fine dining place is open. Do you want to go get something to eat? I'll drive."

"I can drive."

The drive to the diner is short and quiet. Lana holds Georgia's hand on her belly, demanding she be quiet. "You'll scare the baby if you say anything," she whispers. "Did you feel that!?"

Lana looks at Georgia with wide eyes. "Wait, that was her?"

"Yes!" Lana laughs and rubs her belly. "Be nice to your aunt."

"That must feel weird."

Lana shrugs her shoulders. "It did at first but I'm used to it now. You'll know what it's like when you get to experience it."

Georgia laughs, "I don't know if I'll ever experience kids."

"Don't you want kids?"

"I don't have strong feelings about it one way or the other." Truthfully, Georgia has begun to wonder if she's one of those women who will never be married. The idea doesn't sadden her like others would assume. She's happy with her life as it is. She has a great job, a nice home, and good friends. Romance is the only thing she's missing.

"That's because you haven't met the right person."

The sisters walk into the hometown diner and seat themselves at a table in front of one of the large square windows. None of the tables or chairs match which adds to the uniqueness of Ralph's. The walls are painted mint green and there's a speckled white counter with mix-match barstools.

"Nothing has changed," Georgia comments with a soft smile. She lifts the menu and reads over the options. "I've been thinking about this chili for years, but now that I'm here I kind of want a cheeseburger."

Lana chuckles. "That is the magic of this place. Everything tastes good so it's hard to choose. That ritzy place could never."

"Is Leah still working there?" Georgia asks. Leah is one of Lana's closest friends from high school.

"She is. She said she makes decent tips from the professional crowd. I guess that's one good thing about the restaurant coming to town. More of the professional types have been attracted to the town. They like the small-town life after working hard in a big city all day. Maybe you would like it too if you give it a try."

Georgia presses her lips together with humor. "You can keep trying Lana, but I'm not moving back to Golden Shore. Not now at least." As she speaks, the bell above the door chimes signaling someone's arrival. Georgia looks up and her breath catches as she locks eyes with Declan. Recognition covers his face almost as clearly as the facial hair on his angular chin.

He walks over to their table and stands stoically. "Hey Georgia, I didn't know you were in town."

"I could say the same about you. I just got in town today, but I hear you've been here for a couple of months."

He nods his head. "I have. It's good to see you. I guess I'll, uh, see you around."

"Or you could join us," Lana suggests. When Georgia looks at her with wide eyes, she winks.

Declan hesitates, "Are you sure? I don't want to intrude."

"You wouldn't be intruding at all. Right, Georgia?"

Georgia nods her head. "That's right. Pull up a chair." She doesn't have a reason to not want Declan to join them. It's not like they were a couple who ended badly. They were friends, close friends. They just lost touch. Sharing space for one meal won't hurt her.

"So, how does it feel to be back home, Declan?" Lana asks after they order their food.

"It feels ... good. I've been away a long time. I'm happy to be here now."

Lana hums and looks pointedly at her sister. "Did you hear that, Georgia?"

"I heard it, Lana."

Declan looks between the two women. "I feel like I'm missing something."

"Lana is trying to get me to move back to Golden Shore," Georgia explains.

"I'm just saying, you've lived in the big city long enough. It's time to come back to your roots."

"Where do you live?"

"Atlanta."

"I spent some time there before I was stationed in the Middle East."

Georgia's eyes widen. "You were on the frontlines?"

Declan stiffly nods and scratches his chin. "I was a part of WARCOM for a few years."

"Thank you for your service." Lana and Georgia say simultaneously.

Declan clears his throat. "So, Georgia, how long are you in town for?"

"A week," she answers. "Long enough to celebrate Christmas with my family."

"A few of us from high school are getting together tonight for a game of softball. You should join us."

She giggles and shakes her hand. "You know I've never been good at that sport, but I'll watch from the bleachers."

"That'll work."

Having lunch with Declan isn't as awkward for Georgia as she thought it may be. The two old friends talk and joke like they used to. Lana joins in their chatter, but she mostly observes them. It's almost like she's trying to figure something out. Georgia doesn't know what it could be.

Declan surprises them when he takes out his wallet and places enough money on the table to cover all of their meals. "Thanks for letting me join you."

"Oh, you don't have to pay for our meals."

"I know I don't have to, but I want to," he counters.

"Well, at least stay so we can buy you dessert."

"I wish I could but, I've been working at the hardware store with my Dad and I'm late for my shift. I'll see you tonight Georgia." He walks out of the diner before she can respond.

Lana smirks. "Wow. That was like watching a Netflix rom-com."

Georgia's eyebrows furrow. "What are you talking about?"

"You'll figure it out soon," she says with confidence. Something tells her that Georgia will be spending more than a week in Golden Shore.

To say that Declan was surprised to see Georgia would be an understatement. It would also be a lie to say that he hasn't been wondering if he would see her since he's been back in Golden Shore. He still remembers the last time he saw her like it was yesterday. She rode with him and his parents to the airport when he left to report for basic training. He remembers her crying and making him promise to keep in touch. At first, he did, then they grew apart. He can't point to any one thing that led to their lack of communication. It just happened. They both started missing calls and eventually stopped calling altogether. Now with her back in town, he wonders if they may be able to pick up where they left off. Maybe they'll even be able to develop something more.

~~*~~

Georgia paces her old room while she watches the clock. She thinks about canceling so she can stay home with her sister and watch old Christmas movies, but before she can pull her phone out to send Declan a text, there's a knock on the front door.

"Georgia! Declan's here!" Her mom, Stacy, calls up the stairs.

"Coming!" Georgia gives herself a once-over in the mirror and runs down the stairs. She's wearing jeans, a brown cropped sweatshirt, and Timberland boots. Declan is standing in front of the door wearing a long-sleeved plain white t-shirt with an unbuttoned baseball jersey and black sweatpants. "What are you doing here?"

"I figured we could carpool." He shrugs his wide shoulders. "Are you ready to go?"

"Um, yeah. I guess so." It's too late to back out now. He's here and expecting her to follow through with their plans. She grabs her black puffy coat from the hook and follows Declan outside. There's a shiny black pick-up truck parked along the curb. He opens the passenger door for her.

"Nice ride," she comments when he's sitting behind the steering wheel.

He chuckles, "I drove this thing all the way from Washington and I don't mean D.C."

"Impressive."

The light mood lasts throughout the drive to the baseball field. Climbing out of Declan's truck and stepping onto the gravel ground causes a rush of memories from high school to flood Georgia's mind. She spent many mornings, afternoons, and weekends sitting on the uncomfortable metal bleachers as she watched Declan play his favorite sport. Tonight is very reminiscent of those days. Most of the people here are people who were either on the team with Declan or on the softball team.

To nobody's surprise, Declan and his team win the game. The few people in the stands rush the field to congratulate the winners. Declan runs up to Georgia and picks her up in a spinning hug.

"Congrats!" She laughs as he puts her down. "I had no doubts that you'd win."

"Hmm, so that wasn't you that was panicking over the rest of the crowd when we were down three points?"

Georgia taps her chin in thought. "I do not recall."

He chuckles and hugs her. "It was nice having you here. It felt like..."

"...like old times."

"Yeah," He smiles down at her. "Hey, um... if you're not doing anything on Christmas night, do you want to go to the Christmas festival downtown?"

"Absolutely."

"Good. Good."

She giggles as she looks up at him. "'Good. Good?' Your vocabulary hasn't improved all these years. I guess some things never change."

"Kind of like how I play better when you're watching."

"Is that so?"

"Yeah, it is." He rubs a hand over his silky hair. "What would you say to spending some time together while you're in town?"

Georgia's easy smile slips. "Um, I would say that's unexpected."

"Is it really?" Declan questions while sitting on the metal bench. He pats the space beside him.

"Yeah, it is, really. We haven't talked to each other in years."

"I am well aware. We have a lot of catching up to do."

"Why?"

He puffs out a breath. "You said before that my vocabulary isn't any good. The truth is there are so many things I wish I would have said to you before I left, but I never said them."

Georgia gulps and rubs her hands together. "Things like what?"

"Like how I've been in love with you since we were eleven. Like how my entire time in the military, all I could think about was when I'd get to see you next. Like how since we lost touch, I've been kicking myself for letting you go."

"Declan," Georgia breathes and places her hand on his knee. "I don't plan on staying in town after Christmas is over."

"Then we make the most of our time while you're here. After the week is over, we see where we stand and where we want to go from there."

"And you're okay with the possibility of me leaving and not coming back?"

"Who said I won't follow you?"

Her heart skips a beat. "Really?"

"Maybe. We'll see. What do you say?" Georgia leans forward and gives Declan a soft kiss.

"I say I'm so glad I came home for the Holidays."

Geekmas

Tori can't believe her bad luck. Just as she's getting used to one school, her parents pack up and move her to another city in another state. She's so tired of moving. She can't be too mad at them, though. Her dad is a co-owner of a prominent hotel chain. He was presented with a new business opportunity two months ago that is requiring them to move two weeks before Christmas. He promised her this was the last time they'd move, but he said that the last time and the time before that. This is their third move in two years. She's basically given up on making friends. What's the point when she'll just leave again?

As they drive through their new hometown, Tori can't help but notice how much smaller it is compared to where they've been living. There's an actual circle with a gazebo. It reminds her of Stars Hallow from *Gilmore Girls*. She's excited to get to be a part of the small-town life, but also nervous. She's coming into the semester late. People are going to leave for winter break knowing her only as the 'new girl.'

"You'll have to get to school early Monday so you can get your schedule."

"Can't I just wait until next semester?" Tori asks her dad as they pull up to their new house.

"Tori, you know we can't let you do that." He sighs and puts the car in park. "We don't want you to be more behind on the curriculum here than you already are."

"Dad, please. I don't want to go this late. I'd only be missing a few days. Is that really such a bad thing?" The small family gets out of the car and walks into their new home. The movers her parents hired have already unpacked and set the house up for them.

"I can't have this argument again," he groans and looks at his wife. "Rebecca, please talk to her." Tori rolls her eyes as her dad walks upstairs to find his new home office. He tends to 'hand off' conversations to Tori's mother when he's done talking.

"Tori, as much as I'd love for you to stay home tomorrow, you know you can't. Your dad is right." Her mom wraps her in a delicate hug and kisses the top of Tori's head. "Maybe I can check you out from school early on Friday so you can help me decorate the Christmas tree."

"Okay," Tori sighs and finally returns her mom's hug. "Which room did you say is mine?"

"Up the stairs, third door on the left." Tori nods and drags herself up the stairs. After finding her bedroom, she flops down on the bed and stares up at the ceiling.

Tori hates being the new girl. Everyone always stares, and once they find out she's a member of *the* Whitmore family, it all goes downhill. They all want to hang out with her because their parents need jobs, or they want a friend with money, and it gets old really quick.

The only person who ever really understood where she came from was her best friend Chelsea. She's also from a pretty prominent family and her mom is another co-owner of the hotels. The two girls became fast friends over the past two years. Tori hasn't been able to see Chelsea in a little over a year due to the pair always moving around, but they have plans to see each other over the New Year and Tori couldn't wait.

"So where are you now?" Chelsea asks as Tori tries to rearrange her room the way she likes it.

"Some small town. Golden Shore, Virginia." Tori groans as she moves her bed against her wall. "Small town, but it's a nice change of pace."

"You sound like your dad."

"Gross," Tori laughs and moves over to the wall with a built-in bookshelf. "The movers did an *awful* job at arranging my books. They put all the classics with my vampire series."

"Oh *no*. Whatever will you *do?!*" Chelsea gasps in mock horror.

"Oh, shut up." Tori looks back at her open laptop with the video call on and gives her friend the middle finger.

"Just so you know, I screenshotted that and I'm sending it to your dad."

"Oh, please. Like he'll care. Just don't post it online. Can't have his 'rebellious teenage daughter' ruining his image of this perfect family," Tori mutters and sits at her desk in front of the laptop. "I'm gonna try and get some sleep. Long day tomorrow with the first day of school and all."

"Call me if you need me, okay? Love you."

"Love you." Tori sighs and shuts her computer. She takes a look around her room, mentally planning out how she's going to rearrange it and decorate it over the Christmas break. She doesn't know how long she'll live here, but the space where sleeps should at least have personal touches.

~~*~~

Her mom drops her off at the entrance of the school the next morning and leans over the passenger seat to wish Tori luck on her first day. "Call me if you need me."

"What if I want to come home?" Tori adjusts the strap of her backpack on her shoulder.

"Give it until lunch period at least." Her mom practically begs her. "I know it's hard, but I think you'll like it here once you get used to it."

"It's not that I won't get used to it, it's that I'd rather wait until after the break is over."

"I know, honey. But your father... you know how he is. This week will fly by. You went to one of the top high schools in the country before coming here. You won't be behind, if anything you'll be ahead of your other classmates. You're going to be great. I love you."

"Love you too, mom." Tori mutters and turns to enter the building.

The school is small and packed with kids trying to make it to the cafeteria for breakfast before the first bell rings. The front office is located about ten steps inside the building once stepping through the entrance. Most of the classrooms are located in the same hallway with the office smack in the middle.

Tori makes her way into the office (after bumping into six different kids) and introduces herself to the secretary. "Hi, I'm Victoria Whitmore. I need to pick up my schedule."

"Yes, yes. Of course. We've been expecting you." The small woman shuffles through a stack of papers. "Here we are. We got your transcripts from your previous school three days ago and made up your schedule the best we could. You'll exceed in all of the classes we put you in, so not to worry." She hands Tori her schedule. "Now, here's a map of the school. Most everything is in this hall aside from your science class. That's located in the building outside. Your first three classes are at the very end of the hall here," She circled three doors on the map in pink highlighter. "Then you have your science class in the science building. After that, you have lunch in this building over here. Then your last three classes are at the other end of the hall down here." Tori nods and looks over the map. It seems simple enough to understand. "Oh, and that's the bell. Have a good first day, Victoria."

"Thank you," Tori smiles and leaves the small office to try and make it to her first class.

She's relieved to be the first to arrive to the class, and even more relieved when her math teacher tells her the only open seat is in the back corner of the room. She takes her seat and pulls out a notebook and pen.

A scrawny boy with bright orange hair stumbles his way to the back of the class and nearly drops all his books as he takes his seat. He notices the seat next to him is occupied for the first time all year and immediately avoids eye contact with the stranger. The last thing he needs is another person trying to make fun of him.

"Hi," His ears perk up when he hears her speak. "I'm Tori." The pretty girl is smiling at him.

"Eddie." He replies shortly and gets his notebooks and pens out.

"Do you know what section we're supposed to be on? It's my first day and I don't want to be flipping through and trying to figure out what page we're on."

"Oh, um, chapter 11, section 16." Eddie mumbles and flips his own textbook open. Tori decides to give up on trying to converse with him and opens her new textbook to chapter eleven. As soon as class is over, Eddie packs his bag as quickly as he can and rushes out of the room, tripping over his own feet on the way out.

"Hey! I'm Taylor. Need any help finding your next class?" A girl with light brown hair and glasses framing her face offers to Tori when she's finished packing her backpack.

"Oh, no thank you. It's just across the hall." Tori smiles at the kind offer.

"Oh, that's my next class, too! Mind if I walk with you?"

"Not at all." The two walk in silence across the hall.

"Hey, the seat next to me has been empty all semester if you want to sit there," Taylor offers. "The only other seat open is beside Eddie. You may not want that one though."

"Why? Is he not a nice guy?"

"Oh, no, it's nothing like that. There's nothing wrong with him, he's just... odd."

"Yeah, I noticed. I sat next to him in the last class." Tori clears her throat and takes the seat next to Taylor. "Is he always that... off?"

"Not always. He's actually super cool when he's able to relax. He's on the track team."

"Are you talking about the scrawny ginger who tripped when he was walking out of the classroom?"

"Yep, I am. He's the star of the track team because he's their secret nuclear weapon. Nobody really knows how though. He's got asthma and can't walk more than three steps without tripping. He doesn't run often, but he's won every race he's ever ran."

"He doesn't look like he'd be on the track team," Tori looks back at the scrawny kid as he arranges his pens on his desk.

"Believe it or not, he's actually pretty athletic. He's fast and strong. It's so weird." Tori raises an eyebrow. "I mean, you gotta squint, tilt your head to the left, and close your right eye to see any muscle... but it's there." Tori squints her eyes to try and see it, but before she can tilt her head the bell rings indicating that class has started.

The rest of the school day goes by pretty quickly as Tori learns her way around the school. The only issue she really has all day is finding the cafeteria, but even that isn't as difficult as she initially thought it would be. When her mom pulls up to the front of the school, Tori jumps in the passenger seat and smiles over at her mom.

The woman is surprised to see her daughter in such a good mood. "Good first day, then?" She asks as they pull out of the school parking lot.

"Yeah, it wasn't too bad." Tori shrugs. "I met a couple of girls named Taylor and Elizabeth. Their sisters and their parents own some high-end restaurant in town that a lot of people hate. I have two classes with Taylor, her sister has lunch with us. A lot of people stared at me, but that's nothing new."

"How were your classes?"

"Not bad. Everyone is going over their exam reviews right now, so I've only got reviews to do. It seems like most of what will be on the exams is stuff I learned at my old school. The week should be super easy, but I still would have rather waited until next semester to begin."

"I tried talking to your father about it, but he's set in his ways. If you finish all your exams early on Friday, I can still check you out so we can decorate. That's only if you want."

"Yes, please. Can we decorate my room, too?"

"Of course. I've already got your three-foot tree out and ready to be put up in your room."

"You're the best, Mom. Your husband, Arthur, needs to try more."

"Tori, be respectful. You and he may not be seeing eye to eye right now, but he's still your dad."

Tori scoffs and rolls her eyes. "Mom, you've basically been a single parent my whole life. Dad has never been interested in me."

"That's not true. He's just busy with the hotels."

"Chelsea's mom co-owns the hotels and her dad is a surgeon, but they spend time with her. Face it, Dad doesn't care what I do so long as it doesn't ruin the perfect family public image that he's cultivated."

Rebecca frowns as she listens to her daughter. She hates that Tori feels that way, but she can understand why she does. Arthur has always been a distant father. He provides everything Tori could want and need financially, but he doesn't often give emotional support. The role of caretaker and listening ear has always fallen on Rebecca's shoulder alone. She hates that her daughter doesn't know what it's like to have a close relationship with her dad. That's one of the reasons she pushed so hard for him to expand the hotels to a small town like Golden Shore. Rebecca's hope is that being here will allow her husband to slow down and take notice of what he has in life. She's already told him that she won't let him uproot Tori again. It's not fair. The girl is a sophomore in high school and she's moved more than any other teenager. Golden Shore will be their home at least until Tori goes to college. It's time for the girl to live like a normal American teenager.

~~*~~

The rest of the week passes by without incident. Tori is determined to break Eddie out of his shell. She doesn't know why, but something about him is interesting. He's a conundrum. It's obvious that he's popular with the other students, but he walks around as if he has no clue. He's polite to her, but their conversations never last long. On the days that Taylor and Elizabeth are finished with their exams and get to go home early, Tori sits with Eddie at lunch. The first time she does it, he ignores her. By the second time, he seems stiff with anticipation. It's obvious he's getting a little more comfortable around her when the week comes to an end.

On Friday, she only has her first-period class exam, so it's going to be an early day for her. She has already covered all the material at her previous school the year prior, so she's one of the first people to finish the exam. Well, she and Eddie finish at about the same time.

"Thank you, Tori. Eddie. You may go." Their teacher dismisses them without hesitation. The two return to their desks to pack their things before walking out of the classroom.

"See you in the new year," Eddie mumbles as they walk down the hall towards the entrance.

"Hey, do you want to go with me to the cafe downtown?" She offers when they step outside the school.

"Why? Are uh, are all your friends still inside?" He asks, digging through his backpack for his cell phone.

"You're my friend, too. And no, I just thought we could hang out outside of school for a change." She shrugs her shoulders. Eddie looks up with his hand curled around his phone. "So, what do you say? It's a ten-minute walk, right?"

"Um, yeah. Yeah, okay." Eddie agrees and stuffs his phone in his pocket.

"You'll have to slow down. I can't keep up with you, long legs," Tori teases and falls into pace beside him. "What are your plans for the break?" She asks, but he doesn't respond. "My family isn't doing much. I'm helping my mom decorate the tree today whenever I get home. Dad probably won't be home for Christmas aside from the morning to open presents and take pictures, but that's nothing new. He'll probably have business meetings. Right before New Year's a friend of mine is flying in to visit, so that'll be fun. If you're free, you're welcome to join us. We probably won't be doing much aside from eating junk food and watching the ball drop."

"You don't have plans to do something extravagant, then?" He asks, slowing his pace as best he could to not pass her too far.

"No, we went to New York for the ball drop last year, but that's the most 'extravagant' thing we've done for the holidays. Dad tries to keep the 'simple life' family image, which isn't a bad thing. I really enjoy not going on big trips. Christmas should be family time."

"Yeah, I totally agree." He clears his throat. "I'd actually really like to join you and your friend for New Years if that's okay."

"Of course it is."

"Thank you. Nobody ever really invites me to do anything." He sheepishly admits.

"What? There's no way that's true. Just this week alone I saw seven different girls ask you out on dates." Eddie comes to a dead stop on the sidewalk. "You... you didn't notice that you were being asked out?" His face turns bright red and he starts walking towards the cafe again. "Oh, hey, Eddie, it's okay! You don't need to be embarrassed! Lots of people don't realize when they're being asked out!" Tori has to jog to catch up to the tall boy.

"I'm not embarrassed," Eddie sighs and holds the cafe door open for Tori. "I just never thought anyone would want to actually go out with me."

"What are you talking about?" Tori looks up at him bewildered. "Why would they not?"

"I don't know. I kind of just figured they wanted to hang out because I've got good grades and would help them with their projects or homework. I never thought they'd actually want to hang out with me for me."

"Well, I like hanging out with you." Tori nudged him as they went to find an empty table. "I think you're pretty cool, actually." Eddie's face turns red and he bumps into an empty chair, tripping over the leg. "Are you okay?"

"Yeah, yeah. I'm okay." He clears his throat and leans on the chair. "Is this table okay?"

"Absolutely." She smiles as Eddie takes a seat. "Do you want a hot chocolate?"

"Yeah, hold on, let me get my wallet out."

"Oh, no need. I invited you, so the least I can do is pay." She shrugs and walks up to the counter to order their drinks. "Two of those brownies too, please." As soon as their order is up, Tori walks it over to their table. *"Bon appetite*, or however you say it."

"Thank you," Eddie smiles and reaches for his hot chocolate. Tori pushes one of the brownies towards him and begins sipping on her drink. "So... um, would it be too forward if I asked for your phone number? I've never asked for a girl's number before, so I don't know if--"

"Yes, Eddie you can have my number." Tori laughs and holds her hand out for his phone. He hands it over and Tori puts in her phone number and calls her own phone. "Now I have your number, too."

"Cool." He clears his throat and takes his phone back. "So um, now what?"

"Now we hang out and get to know each other, become better friends... maybe more, if that's something you're interested in?"

"Yes," Eddie answers a little too quickly. "Yes, I'd love to maybe be more than friends."

Tori smiles down at the table and the two continue to chat over their drinks. She can see herself enjoying her time here in Golden Shore with Eddie.

By Christmas, they're planning a date to the town's Christmas light show, where they share a kiss under the mistletoe.

THE END

Are you still looking for something to read? Keep reading for sneak peeks of other books released by Free Minds Publications, then visit our website!

www.freemindspublications.com

FREE MINDS PUBLICATIONS PRESENTS

The Positivity Verses

L. J. STEED

The Positivity Verses

L. J. Steed

Words

All these words all these words

They're just words of boredom and dull.

Words of sadness

To
dis
pel
the
ba
dn
ess

To
bel
ay
the
ma
dn
ess

The madness of these words.

Here it is and here they sit

Penned and penciled in

In penciled blackness

To express the sadness

To belay the madness

The madness of these words

All these words all these words

To try and talk about him or her

To
bel
ay
the
dar
kne
ss

To
blu
nt
the
sha
rpn
ess

The sharpness of their words.

FREE MINDS PUBLICATIONS PRESENTS
DAN MAINWARING
THE TREACHEROUS EXHIBIT
A HISTORICAL MYSTERY

THE TREACHEROUS EXHIBIT

Daniel Mainwaring

CHAPTER 1

A Warm Beverage For The Deceased

"This 'Viennese coffee' tastes an awful lot like chicory and dandelion. Are you serving up sludge from the Thames?" The patron asked impudently as he shoved his mug across the table. Henry Sacker was mortified. He had worked tirelessly to maintain his coffee shop's highbrow reputation. But worse than the customer's attitude was his hauntingly familiar face.

"I thought you were dead."

The man laughed. "Not dead, just lost at sea! A convenient way to escape a wearisome marriage." Sacker slid into the wooden chair opposite his customer. Just ten years earlier the duo were work colleagues.

Sacker responded, "I was surprised when I read an obituary for Owen Johns in The Times. I puzzled how the devil himself could be dead." Johns chuckled at Sacker's deadpan remark.

"You flatter me, Henry," he said. "Rogue, blaggard perhaps. But 'Devil'? That's a title I merely aspire to."

Age hadn't been kind to Owen Johns. He was a well-kept, dark-haired, statuesque man when he first encountered Henry in 1841. They crossed paths in Hyderabad while working for the East India Company.

Johns was from aristocratic Irish stock. His family had embraced the protestant reformation and in the process gained additional property from their catholic neighbors. As a rebellious teenager, Johns left home and joined the merchant navy. The East India Company offered him further adventure with greater rewards and fewer risks.

Unlike Johns, Sacker sought conformity and a sense of belonging. His father, a German Jew, had left Prussia as antisemitic sentiment arose at the start of the century. As a refugee in London, with little money but a deft touch for sewing, he established himself as a tailor in Bethnal Green.

By the time Henry reached adulthood, Sacker senior was a moderately wealthy merchant. Henry, heavily anglicized at school, felt a deep sense of gratitude towards his family's adopted home. He joined the civil service at 18 before being offered an administrative role for the East India Company. The private corporation and the state were virtually indistinguishable.

Sacker never felt he had really left the civil service. Olive skinned, slightly built, and short-sighted, he was visually as well as physically the opposite of Johns. But despite Johns' rough exterior, he was astute enough to identify Sacker's intelligence, industriousness, and loyalty. He seconded his young colleague into a semi-official role working for the British Foreign Office. They were to safeguard government interests in India.

For a time things worked well. Sacker established cordial relationships with the native population and surreptitiously gathered information on potential threats. Of particular concern at the time were sophisticated gangs of bandits known as thuggee. They preyed on naive travelers, befriending them and aiding their travel before robbing and murdering them.

Sacker made contact with a Brahman former thuggee named Mishra who had since gained work as a courier. Sacker convinced Mishra to infiltrate a thuggee group in Etawah. The gang regularly looted company storehouses and killed British settlers. Using intelligence from Sacker, Johns organized a late-night raid on the bandits' camp. It descended into violence and chaos. All the thuggee were killed, including Mishra.

THE DIFFERENCE

YOU HAVE MADE

BY JAY QUIN

THE DIFFERENCE YOU HAVE MADE

By Jay Quin

Chapter 1

The Escape

SMACK! The large brown hand strikes the unsuspecting face. The force knocks her into the wood-paneled wall. Slowly she slides to the concrete floor. Her shaking almond hand clutches her throbbing right cheek.

"Now I'm going to work angry because of you!" The tall man yells as he stands over her with a dark and menacing look on his square face. His thick eyebrows are raised high on his slopped forehead. A vein throbs in his forehead right between his eyes. He's angrier than she's ever seen him before, and she's seen him be angry *a lot*.

Desperately, she tries to calm him down. "Tyson, I didn't mean to upset you."

"Shut up!" He seethes, snatching his red windbreaker jacket off the back of the wicker dining chair and stomping out of the dilapidated apartment. Anxiously she listens for the sound of his heavy footsteps descending the creaky staircase. When she's sure he's gone, she carefully stands to her feet. She learned long ago that if she moves too fast after one of his attacks, it'll only make her suffering worse.

Despair hangs over her head like a dark cloud as she makes her way to the dented white refrigerator. Inhaling deeply, she grabs a handful of ice and pours it into a plastic bag. She holds the bag to her stinging cheek. There's no denying it, it is past time for her to make a run. The cruelty that Tyson routinely subjects her to has tainted her life for entirely too long. She used to think that things would get better, but it's been over four months already and there's no sign that anything will change. The man who was once her loving boyfriend no longer exists. He's been replaced by an abusive and controlling tyrant. It started with demeaning words meant to tear down her confidence. When that no longer worked, he escalated to physical assaults. Now she spends every day worrying that it will be her last. She hardly sleeps at night because she's scared to let her guard down when he's around. She's at the mercy of his violent and erratic temperament. It's not safe.

You don't have to put up with this anymore. You can get out. The thought is like a bright sign flashing in her mind as she remembers the job advertisement that she saw online the night before.

LIVE-IN NANNY NEEDED

All applicants must be female and have at least one year of childcare experience. Serious candidates will have to undergo a background check and drug screening. This position requires you to live on-site and provide full-time care to a two-year-old boy. Walk-in interviews will be available Tuesday, August 11th from 8 AM until 1 PM at 1231 Enterprise Avenue, Suite 1012. Ask for Rachel Skylark. A resume is required.

She paces on the dingy carpet flooring of the small square living room, contemplating what could be a way for her to finally escape this never-ending nightmare. Any other job would require her to work secretly for months to save even half of the money she needs to move out. If she's hired for *this* job, it will give her a new home right away. The need to get away from Tyson grows stronger every day. His vicious attacks are intensifying. It's only a matter of time before he sends her to the hospital, or worse, kills her.

There's no guarantee that she'll be chosen for the job, but it's a step in the right direction. Besides, there will be no harm done no matter the outcome. If she is hired, then she'll be able to leave without her so-called boyfriend interfering. If she isn't hired, then Tyson will never know that she's trying to get away from him. It's a win-win situation, something she rarely encounters anymore.

Her eyes move to the digital clock of the microwave. It's just after nine o'clock in the morning. Tyson won't be home from work until after six. There's plenty of time for her to go to the interview and return home. A slow grin spreads across her diamond-shaped face. She's going to do it. She's going to the interview for the job. It's exciting and nerve-racking.

Quickly the grin falls as a nearly pained groan sounds from her mouth. The disheartening reminder that she's without transportation flashes in her mind. Again, she paces as she thinks of a way around the hole in her plan. This situation will not be the end of her. She will not die at the hands of a cowardly man like Tyson. She will escape, even if she must walk to her first glimpse of freedom.

FREE MINDS PUBLICATIONS PRESENTS

Sarah's
New Beginning
Tammy Anderson

SARAH'S NEW BEGINNING

Tammy Anderson

Chapter One

August 1837

As Sarah Whitfield sat looking out the window of the moving train, her mind drifted back to the week before when her journey began. She could almost feel the memories; they were so strong in her mind. As far back as Sarah could remember she had lived at the orphanage under the care of Joanne Stiltner. Miss Stiltner was the closest thing to a mother that Sarah had ever known, and she loved her as such. Miss Stiltner had put Sarah in touch with a family who was friends of hers back west. Leaving her had been a very hard task, but Sarah knew she needed a fresh start since coming of age at the orphanage. Knowing Miss Stiltner knew the people to whom she would soon trust her life was the only thing that gave the young girl the courage to leave. The tears began to gather in her eyes as she thought of the last hug from the woman she cared for with such deep feelings.

"I'm so frightened! What if they don't like me?" Sarah had asked desperately.

"They will love you, dear," she assured her.

"But if they don't and they ask me to leave then I'll be all alone," she said with dismay through her tears.

"Sarah, if things don't go well then you are more than welcome to come back to me." Joanne gathered Sarah into her arms and tried to soothe the young girl's fears.

"I can? Really?"

"Really. But I can tell you, Sarah, the Martins are fine Christian people and will not only take care of you, but they will love you. Just as I have come to love and care for you. I have no doubt they will love you. I would not send you if I thought for even a moment you would not be welcomed and loved."

Though the train had carried her hundreds of miles away, Sarah could still feel the strong loving arms of the kind woman around her. Joanne Stiltner had held onto Sarah a long time that day to reassure her all would be fine. Sarah was thankful for the love she felt and carried with her because of this dear friend. She trusted and loved her as she never had another. Leaving her was the hardest thing she had ever had to do in her young life. How long would it be before she was able to see her again? If ever again? Sarah shook her head to clear away the thoughts.

Good-byes were not anything new to the young girl, for people had come and gone quite regularly at the home. But this time was different. She was the one who left. Sarah knew she would be crying in earnest if her thoughts continued along that path and again shook her head to clear away the memories that would not give her mind rest. Sarah knew she should be excited over this new venture but felt more frightened than excited as the train carried her farther down the tracks away from the only life she had ever known.

Sarah continued to look out the window at the beautiful landscape passing her by at great speed. They were very different from the start of her journey, gone were the mountains filled with trees and cool running rivers. Oh, how she longed for a cool drink from those rivers. Her mouth was so dry from the heat and dust of her long journey.

Now as she looked about it was a flat terrain. The trees were still there, though not as many. Nor were they as big. It was still beautiful to look about and see the different terrain. She couldn't help but wonder if the land could get any flatter or the trees scarcer as the train continued its Westward destination.

**You can find this and other great books on our website.
www.freemindspublications.com**